P9-EDW-403

The Garden of Eros

For John and Lorri
who helped provide some of
the experience for this one

Ata Books
1920 Stuart Street
Berkeley, California 94703

First Edition
Printed in the United States of America
Library of Congress Catalog Number: 78-73215
ISBN: 0-931688-03-5

Cover design and illustration: Robert Bryant

THE GARDEN

OF

EROS

a novel by
Dorothy Bryant

Ata Books
Berkeley, California

That pain again. Stomach. No. Back? Shifting? Gone. Just gas again. Like this afternoon? Something I ate. Keep holding the candle up high so they see me in the window. Up high like the girl in the myth, holding up the candle to see her lover, her god of love, forbidden, he'll vanish. But I don't see my lover and never will. The candle lights me up for him to see, for Ken. And for Maggie, who must be waving upward to the window even though she knows I can't see her. What does she always say? *The feeling, my dear, might come through even though you don't see me. Is that right or just an old woman's wish?* Yes, right, it does come through, I don't know how. Is Ken waving too? Probably not. He will just be standing looking up at me, not moving on the outside, always still, at attention, in control even when he is churning on the inside.

But Ken's stillness reaches me faster than Maggie's waving. I always feel his attention right away, touching me, checking to make sure I'm still here, needing me, saying I am strong even though I'm not, saying he needs me and that makes it true for a little while, his needing makes me strong. Only for a minute or two. Don't feel it now. There. The car starting. Blow it out. Put it down. Careful. Feel the table. There. Right in the middle. Go on, Ken, drive Maggie to her car and hurry back. No, don't hurry over that road, so scary that Maggie parks her car outside on the highway. *And you told me you drove an ambulance in Spain,* Ken teased but she gave it right back. *That was in 1936 when I was your age, Ken.* And at my age, where were you then? I prompted her, wanting to hear another of her stories. *At your age? Oh, my dear, at twenty-one? Was I ever twenty-one? Yes, at twenty-one I was a veteran of the women's suffrage fight with, I might add, a respectably long arrest record, longer than yours, Ken.* He went tight and mumbled *and for clearer reasons* and then something else I couldn't hear. Then a silence like a minute to remember the dead while I hoped he wouldn't slip into one of his tight, still moods but I knew Maggie wouldn't let him. She can say almost anything to Ken, even teasing him about being so much older than I am and he just teases her back, like the driving, that's all it was, teasing, because he wouldn't let her drive that road. Still wet after last week's rain, first shower of fall but enough to make it slick, slippery clay for a day. Choir people all mentioned it when they came in Friday. *Some road! An initiation rite? to prove us worthy to enter!* We wondered if the road would discourage people and make the whole idea impossible. *Not at all, my dears, it makes them feel terribly remote from everything. Even though you're only five miles off the main road, they must crawl slowly into your wilderness, which is exactly what they want, that feeling.* I hope Maggie was right. She must be. Everything couldn't have gone so well otherwise. Such a perfect weekend, everyone saying they wanted to come back, and the choir director actually making a reservation for *your first open weekend in the spring.* While Ken just stood there holding in his feelings. He'll save them all for me. He'll be back in an hour or two and tell me how it feels to be a complete success. Two hours. Can't just stand here for two hours. Another few minutes and I'll get that pain in my back again or in my legs or start feeling dizzy. Better to do something useful. Plenty to do yet before we leave. A few dishes to wash. One-two-three-four-five steps to the sink and—yes, a few more cups to rinse out. Then the rest of the packing. Then, when I hear the car again, I'll go back to the window and light the candle and stand there as if I never moved, and when he asks if I'm posing for a statue, I'll say yes, the Statue of Liberty and he'll say *You're tall enough* and I'll pretend I still get mad when anyone says how big I am but he'll know I'm pretending and he'll give that high, taut little laugh that turns into a silly giggle because he's so tense most of the time that his laugh gets squeezed out of him like a squeak. No, not so tense now, not the way he was when we first found each other. Not the way I was, tensed up ready to cry, so mad and frustrated and ashamed and scared. I had thought I was doing everything right, swinging the cane across the concrete in front of me, right foot/left cane/left foot/right cane, I had finally got the motion Carol taught me and I knew where I was. Then all of a sudden I didn't know where I was. My cane was hitting something that shouldn't be there, a wall? a rock? and the traffic sounds roared and puffed in front of me, when they'd been behind me just a few steps back so how could this be another street? and more traffic to my right and grass to my left. And I was tired of playing The Game, Carol's game of mobility training. *You have to look at it like a game, a detective game. Sherlock Holmes. Examine the evidence, deduct, elementary, my dear Watson!* I tried to hold her words in my mind but they kept getting pushed out by the fear and the shame and the awful helpless misery that came back a dozen times a day, every time I was stopped by something I could not do. Then I would wish I had never come to Berkeley even if that meant I'd be still sitting on the couch at home, dreaming in the dark with my mother still doing everything for me, a big baby again, and my father saying medical science would develop an operation next month, next year, and leaving things around for me to stumble over as if he thought maybe I was faking, couldn't believe, wouldn't believe, but paced around me like I was a cage he was trapped in. Glad to be away from him, yet standing lost on that street and wishing I had never heard of the Homer Center, thinking I would step out in front of a car rather than go back there, if I could even find my way back there, to admit I'd gotten lost again, and not get any pity, only hear Evelyn laugh. *You want to kill yourself, girl, don't step out in front of a car 'cause you probably only get your ass bumped and live and be in a wheelchair, a blind crip,* which was only what I expected to hear from her because how can one blind person expect pity from another? So I stood there wishing again that I had been killed in the accident instead of knocked on the head and wondering why it had to be me when no one else in the car had a scratch. Playing the old complaints like a worn-out record while the wind started up again, blowing at me, shifting sides, scooping up machine sounds and throwing them at me, moaning, rushing whirls of wind sounds until I knew I stood on the edge of a cliff and a strong wind was trying to pick me up, to grab me and throw me off into a deep, dark chasm where I would fall and fall and I was so tired of trying, alone, all alone forever, that I decided to just let go and let the wind sweep me off and down, down. *You want help.* I wasn't startled, so I must have felt him breathing or sensed him as a shadow, a presence, an obstacle, because on a bright day I still know some light and dark. He must have been watching me for a long time, but not just staring the way people do, not just curious. He must have been afraid, must have known that once he spoke, once he started with me—so we were both afraid. I didn't even speak, just nodded because I was afraid I would cry while he went on talking in that gentle, tight voice. *It's an entrance to a parking lot, and your cane hit that little concrete wall at the opening, but if you swing just to the right a little you'll clear it. No curb. The cars are stopping for you now.* I hesitated and then turned toward him and started to ask him to help me, but he backed off! Usually people don't. They may give me the wrong kind of help and get me into worse trouble but they usually want to help. He held back, even holding his breath. Later he told me how he felt, dizzy like me, with a feeling of being, like me, on the edge of a cliff. Then he let go. *Tell me what to do.* Didn't grab or push me the way some people do. Didn't even move. So I took his arm just above the elbow, the way Carol taught me. A funny, unfriendly hold, a kind of pinching grip on the back of the arm, the best way to take a stranger's arm, keeping control, holding instead of letting him wrap my limp arm over his. I held his thin, taut arm and felt he was tall, about six feet, nearly my height. Scratchy wool shirtsleeve with a moldy smell from wherever he lived, some damp old room? Walking pace steady and straight, tight, quiet, light, long steps. He didn't say a word but after we crossed the driveway we kept walking together until I heard the music, the cello, off to the left, over the grass, onto the campus. Later Ken said I stopped *as if struck by an invisible shower of sparks that lit up your face.* That was the way music had begun to feel. I never listened before when I could see. Not really. I did what all the other kids in high school did, turned on the radio station they did, tried to keep the same rhythm they did. Couldn't. Failed the way I always did, always keeping up an imitation of being normal, an imitation that didn't fool anyone. It wasn't until I came to the Homer Center that I started listening, opening to music. They gave me a tape recorder with a cassette someone had forgotten to take off. At first it was like a thin spear that pierced me and then like threads weaving through me and then I was like a spider with the thread coming out of me, weaving a web, and then I was gone and there was nothing but the threads of music, no me at all, nothing, and I was the music. I still am sometimes when I really listen well. That first time it was viola music by Bach and it came at that special, lost, unhinged time when I was new to The Center, just when I was ready for it. So accidents like leaving that tape on the machine aren't really accidents. Nothing that's happened to me for a long time seems accidental. Everything seems like a step to another step to what I'm ready for. Maggie said it. *All sorts of things offer themselves, and we notice just one, the one we can use.* It was like that with the cello, sending out that warm coil to wrap around me, around us. *That'll be Celia. Want to go and listen?* Of course, Ken knew her the way he knew all the people who hung out on the campus and Telegraph Avenue, and they all knew him. I nodded, and we turned off to the left, across grass, coming nearer and nearer to the sound until we were almost on top of it, where Ken stopped. *Grass seems dry here.* I let go of his arm and sat down to listen till the music stopped and Celia spoke in a low, throaty, cello voice. *Warm for January. Not enough change to add up to a dollar. People aren't as generous anymore. Everything's different. Know what? I've decided to take that teaching job back in Minnesota. Going home.* Ken didn't say a word, only made little sounds back in his throat to show he was listening. *You have to go home sometime. When are you going home, Ken?* He waited such a long time I thought he would never answer. I could feel him tensing. That was the first time I ever did that, felt without hearing or touching, the feeling of another person, and it came at me so strong that I almost thought it was my own tension. Then I knew it was Ken tightening up and I waited to hear him say why. *I am home.* Sad, angry whisper. Nothing more. His tension seemed so tight that it must break out, but he didn't let it, lips closing over a mouthful of feelings, everything stopped and held until Celia broke in. *Introduce me to your friend.* There was another silence, with Ken holding his breath as if afraid to know me, afraid to get closer. *I don't know her name.* So I told the old story of my name, Ceylon, the exotic name my mother picked for her third daughter, maybe hoping I'd be special, but I didn't turn out to be exotic, just big and awkward so that most people called me Lonnie. Then I closed up too, thinking I'd said too much, remembering how I'd learned my mother would rather have been in Ceylon or any other far place, any place but a housing tract in San Jose, having me ten years after she quit having children. *Ten years before abortion was legal.* She said that only once, then she closed up too because she knew it sounded awful to me. Now it didn't sound so awful because in my head I had been rehearsing it, to tell it as a funny story, being named after a runaway fantasy, a funny story, the way Evelyn was always telling jokes on herself, cruel jokes, sad things that had happened to her that she could always turn into funny, angry stories coming out with a rough laugh that spilled out all the hurt so it scattered harmless into the air. But I was still rehearsing and I suppose I am still rehearsing, never able just to talk, just to let everything out. Not that I'm like Ken. He stops the words because they've all been used before, he's tired of them and mistrusts them. No, I would love to be able to just let out what I'm thinking and not feel silly or stupid or stumbling around to find words to match what starts to form inside. *Shyness is something you outgrow.* Meaning my kind of quiet is different from his. Yes, I knew it even then, while we were sitting there and Celia started playing again and I halfway slipped into the music and felt Ken's tension loosening, turning into alertness, attention focused on me so strongly that I suddenly felt powerful, not shy at all but ready to stand tall and not try to hide my height. Getting up to leave, feeling, hearing him move and expecting him to follow me. But he didn't. He stopped himself, held himself back, tight, watching me, glad I was going, relieved. Yet still watching me as I crossed the grass, touched sidewalk, turned left and headed up Bancroft toward the Homer Center as surely as if I'd always done it alone, feeling strong, feeling him watching, until I turned the corner and the cold wind hit me again as if I'd left the sunlight there on the grass with him. But even the wind didn't seem as cold as it had been because

Cramp? Probably from leaning up against the sink. There. Lean away and it's better. There. Gone. I can't get close to anything anymore. Belly-up to the kitchen sink and I'm still a mile away. Ken laughs when I say it though he usually worries too much about me to laugh. He's glad and he knows I'm healthy and the baby must be strong because it lets me know, kicks out, fights back if it feels crowded like when I push up against the sink. But Ken would have chosen to wait longer to have a baby. If he could have chosen. I never gave him any choice. I made the choice without telling him, without telling myself I was making it, without a plan, without even a thought. I lied the first time we made love when he asked what we should do not to have babies. I lied without it feeling like lying, saying I took care of that, when I hadn't. So I chose Ken before I knew I was choosing while he must have known something because he was always saying *no* to questions I didn't know I was asking, always running away. Even by the time we were together every day, by the time we made our first trip up here, I was still sure we wouldn't be together long. I thought I expected nothing. I thought I'd just go home when my classes at the Homer Center were over, ending just after what I thought would be our first and last trip up here. How long had we known each other? Weeks, only weeks. When Maggie offered us her Mendocino house for a weekend, I thought it would be our last weekend, a last beautiful weekend and then I would just disappear the way I thought he wanted me to. It seems years ago, that weekend, and here we are packing up to go into Mendocino again to wait for the baby and to spend the winter after it's born. Rather stay here in our own place, crude as it still is. Too crude for a new baby even though Ken worked so hard all summer, did so much. Next year. He promised next year we'll try it right through the winter if he manages to get the road fixed before the rains start. Stop dreaming about next year, stop standing around. More packing. Not much more to do, our few clothes, things for the baby. That's all we'll need at Maggie's house and I could get most of it packed before Ken gets back. He'd only need to look around to see what I missed and we could leave tonight. No, another day's work cleaning up outside. And he wouldn't want to drive that road again in the dark. No, we'll leave in bright sunlight, like the first time we drove in to find our place with no idea that we were looking for it but needing to get out of Mendocino after the first day. *It smells of garbage.* Ken was right, there was a kind of rotting smell in the air, no worse than Berkeley or any town but it seemed worse there in the open by the sea. *Something about the tides.* Ken showed me the place where people used to dump garbage off the cliff right opposite Main Street and he said that the garbage chute was gone. *But somehow the smell lingers.* It hung in the thick, warm fog that made everything so still, muffled everything, even the ocean, until a fresh, strong wind began to blow the fog wet and cool across our faces. Beautiful, standing on the edge of the cliff and letting the wet wind whip our faces and hearing the roar coming and going below us. Like standing on the edge of the world. Ken took me out on a jagged bunch of rocks jutting out over the water where the wind swept back and forth as if trying to take us off the rocks, and the ocean far down, down below us made deep, grating groans, not roars or splashes but quieter, trapped, waiting sounds. Ken stood behind me with his arms around me so he could talk into my ear and I could hear him above all the noise. *I want to hold on to you . . . some of your strength. . . .* No point in answering him, in trying to talk against the noise, no point in telling him he was wrong to keep saying that, because I'm not strong at all, only big, not strong inside the way he means. *You will be.* There was no answer to that. So I stood there holding his arms around me for what I thought would be the last time, knowing that our baby might be inside me and not feeling brave or strong about that at all, just trying not to think about it, until I shivered and we turned to walk back across the little meadow to Main Street, Ken describing it to me as we walked. *When I was your age, when what remained of the North Beach poets left San Francisco to come up here, and I followed, thinking those guys had something to say besides NO, this building was an old pool hall that Grace West turned into a boarding house where we sat around a pot-bellied stove and played recorders.* Then he was quiet, and when I asked him to describe more of what the street looked like now, he only said, *Just like Telegraph Avenue,* which I had already heard and smelled and then seen through his eyes: people wandering, waiting, begging, selling, waiting, dying, waiting, all in slow motion like moving under murky water. *There's a street like this in every city, even in San Jose. I know them all.* Suddenly he laughed and said he was happy to see that the boutique which had taken over Grace's place had failed. *That's the one thing we're good at, killing a business like that.* His voice died off until I asked if he might want to visit some old friends while we were here. *We have nothing to say to each other anymore. We were only good at saying NO together, and if any of them are still saying NO, it's just as well if I don't see them.* What he meant, I found out later, was that the ones who would be glad to see him still took dope and drank too much and Ken knew, if I didn't yet, that he couldn't take the chance of being with people who drank. He only hinted. *That bar in the next block is the oldest and most successful business here.* Then a rush of words, impatient, urgent. *Let's go, let's drive inland, find some sunlight. There's sure to be sun just a few minutes in from the shore. We'll drive until we see a good place to hike, then park the car and go on foot.* But wherever we drove there were fences and NO TRESPASSING signs so that we rode on and on for a couple of hours, in and out of back roads until we were about to give up and go back into Mendocino. *Let's just try this one.* He turned off onto a wide road that soon started scratchy gravel whispers. Then it narrowed and darkened and stopped whispering and began closing in silently over me. I could feel the wall of rock going up high on my side of the car, but there was light and deep space on Ken's side. He could see and tell me about the valley below on his side, the thick trees with sometimes a glimpse of a stream far down at the bottom. I could hear it swishing up through the tree smells. Then after a while he was as quiet as the wall of rock, as hard, not tense the way he was with people, but watching, concentrating while we moved slower and slower, rocking up and down, with the sound of branches scraping my side of the car and no other sound at all but Ken's breathing, and holding his breath, and breathing, while we—rocked on mules in a caravan, rocking, rocking us as they slowly picked their way along the narrow trail high on the mountainside. Sheer drop down, down the bare rocky cliff's sheer wall, down into the shadows of that dark chasm, down where black waters flowed slowly and deeply in the dark valley where we all must go when—then a huge sigh from Ken. *I'm glad you couldn't see that stretch of road!* A few minutes more of slow rocking before the sun hit the car again and rocks flew under the wheels and we came out into a broad, open place where Ken stopped and I jumped out of the car because I couldn't wait for him to tell me whether it was rocky or smooth or safe. I knew I never felt so safe before and I said, Ken, we're here, and knew we had arrived, finally somewhere, in the right place, like coming home. Ken's feeling was different. He told me later, but I could feel it even then, that tension of his that is like fear. It is fear, why not think so? He always confesses fear, makes it worse than it really is, the way he makes himself out to be worse than he really is. I tell him sometimes that I think he's really afraid of happiness. *Not fear of happiness, more a fear that I'll fail to live up to happiness.* I still don't understand that, just as I didn't understand it then, when we stood there on either side of the car. I could feel tall wet grass on my legs as I stood in the deep shade and heard water running and Ken took my hand silently and held it tight while we walked toward the sound of the water, coming out into sunlight across a flat, grassy meadow, then into sand, and then down to the rock banks of the creek, rushing with high water then, in February. We stood on the edge until the feeling came over me and I started to pull off my clothes. *What are you doing?* But he knew what I was doing, I was going into the water, knowing that although he was pulling back, he'd follow me because he wouldn't let me go alone, though he kept saying, *It'll be like ice!* and it was, and not very deep, only about four feet in that place, so that I crouched, then swam three or four strokes before touching rocks on the other side and then came back again, and grabbed Ken's head and pulled us both completely under the water for a second before we got out to lie on the sunny rocks and get dry. *Why did you do that?* I didn't know why, only knew that I had suddenly felt we must get under, into, become part of the place, sink into it and be taken by it quickly, before we thought. It's too late now! I said and then laughed because I didn't know what I meant. Ken laughed too as we shivered and put on our clothes and went to explore the place, walking back across the meadow to the other side of the car and standing in the shadow of a hill covered with brush and trees. Ken found a little path zigzagging up the slope to the stone cabin clinging to the side of the hill, and then up above it to the other six lean-to cabins with thin wooden walls and tiny windows and wooden bunks hammered into the walls. We climbed up to the highest one, then walked the zigzag path down again, and even then, that first time, I was able to walk the path alone coming down. Narrow, like a little deer path so my feet could fit into it and feel their way so surely that I almost ran down and Ken said I was better on the path than he was. *That's all there is to see, except for an old outhouse. I wonder what the place was used for. Hunters? Maybe sheepherders. I've heard that they used to drive the flocks up here for the spring grass.* We stood still, imagining, almost hearing the sheep on the meadow. *Let's take a look in the stone cabin.* So we came in here. Ken explained how the cabin must have been built with stones hauled up from the creek, cemented together, with a stone floor and corrugated metal roof. A fireplace at one end. One big window. *It must have been taken from an old city schoolroom. Just like the school I attended in San Francisco.* I felt the small panes and the huge outer frame where it was fastened to the wall at the center so that it tipped like a seesaw to open at the top and bottom. At that time of the afternoon a little sun was coming through, making a warm square where we stood in light while he described the view from the window all the way to the creek and the rocky hill on the other side. There was nothing else but the sink with one pipe and no water coming through it. Oh, yes, and that old dusty broad-brimmed hat hanging on the high peg, still there, we kept it for luck, the dago's hat, we called it after we learned people in town called this place Dago Gulch after an Italian railroad worker who hauled stones up from the creekbed a hundred years ago and built this cabin for his wife and children who were coming from Italy, but their ship sank and he went mad and Mr. Romal at the hardware store says, *Nobody since ever made nothing out of Dago Gulch except to keep patching up those stone walls enough so they're still standing, marking a hard luck place if I ever saw one.* No, no, we don't listen to him because I know what I knew on that day when Ken and I stood under that hat in the light of the window and I told Ken maybe the sheepherders would come back soon and he shook his head. *No, there was a FOR SALE sign on the tree where the road forked off the highway.* I didn't dare to say anything because I knew then for sure that this was the place I'd seen in those dreams I started having right after I came to Berkeley, dreams where I stood in an open place, wearing thick yellow work boots, then climbing a narrow winding path up and up and up with someone holding my hand tight and not speaking, saving all breath for climbing. But all I did then was to tuck that secret away beside the secret of the baby, under the other secret that wiped out both of them, the secret that I was going home, that my time was up at the Homer Center so I would leave Ken, the way I thought he wanted me to, the way he was always warning me that he would leave me. I was going to save him the trouble of running away by running away myself, just disappearing, making it easier for both of us. Just the usual old story: I'd come to Berkeley and met a guy on Telegraph Avenue and gone around with him for a while and then gone home again, just like any student in Berkeley, just like any girl who could see, just like

Pain. Like a menstrual cramp except that it comes and then it goes, like a gas pain. And I'm just sitting here on the bed, not standing up and getting a backache, not leaning my stomach against the sink. So it could be a labor pain. It could. But the baby's not due for almost three weeks yet. I had pains like this last week and they went away. That's why, when I felt them again this afternoon, I thought I ate too much of the fruit Maggie brought. That must be it. I just need to go to the outhouse. Doorknob. There. Open the door. Oh, cold, really winter in the air since that rain. And black dark. So dark here in the country away from all the city lights. Even I can tell the difference, a deeper, darker, black air that makes Ken say he knows, a little of the time, a little of what I live, how I feel. But he doesn't really know because the darkness settles down on him suddenly each night and he has no chance to get used to it so that he would be afraid and helpless without a lantern while I almost never feel afraid anymore, not of being blind. I used to be afraid of the old outhouse at first, of being closed up in there with whatever creatures might come in, but now I guess I'm more at home here, creatures and all, and I don't worry about anything but rattlesnakes and we haven't seen one yet. But just to please me Ken located this new outhouse so we could leave the door open and look out through the brush across the meadow, and even if I can't see it, I feel the openness and imagine the sky and hear the birds so that when we're at Maggie's and using a flush toilet again I will miss... rain? Sudden shower. Pouring! This little roof rattles almost as hard as the cabin's metal roof. But tight, no leaks. Ken built well. There. Stopped just as suddenly as it started. Cloud floating past, dropping rain, passing on to...well, I'm sitting here doing nothing but getting cold. My stomach's all right. So it could be that the baby has started coming. Better get back to the house. Back where I'm warmer. Quick. No, be careful going downhill. I wish Ken would hurry up. No, don't hurry on that road. Almost an hour going, another hour coming back, and some time in between to talk. He and Maggie will want to talk for a while. Give them at least an extra hour because they'll have so much to say, going back over so many years because *I've loved him so much longer than you have, my dear.* Shivering. Shut the door quick. But it's not much warmer in here. I could build a fire. Then when Ken gets back from his long talk with Maggie, it will be all warm and bright for us to sit by and have our own talk, all about the weekend and the baby and all the plans for hard work that Ken will be taking on himself because that's what he does with success, either panics and runs from it or buries it under piles of new demands, one on top of another, the same way I'm piling up paper and wood, paper, wood, there! But what if I light this big stack of wood and then have to rush off to the hospital? I'll wait for a while. If there's no pain, it was a false alarm and I can light it. If I get another pain, I'll know that's it, the baby's coming, and I'll meet Ken at the door with my hospital suitcase packed and ready to go, and we'll have to do our talking in the car, the way he and Maggie are doing now. For it's true that she has loved him much longer than I have, not just known him, but loved him. I could hear it in her voice the first time I met her at that concert Ken took me to. That was the second time we saw each other. No. Third. Our second meeting was an accident again, down on Shattuck Avenue where I went—the furthest I'd walked alone from the Homer Center—to buy my boots, the men's work boots I'd wanted for so long and decided to have though I didn't know why I had to have them. *I'm Ken, remember?* Walked with me into the store and watched me try the boots on, quiet until the clerk spoke to him. *Don't you remember me? We were arrested together back in...Jesus, it's almost exactly ten years since*... he went on soft and wistful while Ken stayed quiet and the man's voice got louder with a hard, bitter ragged edge. *Well, I'm into money now, man, I got a house down The Peninsula with a swimming pool and*.... All at once his voice choked off and he just sighed. So I bought the boots and wore them back to The Center, Ken walking along just half a step behind me as if he didn't want to follow, then leaving me at The Center without a word, so that I was surprised when he called the next day and asked if I wanted to go to a concert on campus, at Hertz Hall. I said I'd been wanting to go there but still hadn't after six months in Berkeley and he said he hadn't been there for years and started to explain all the acoustical reasons why it was a good concert hall. Friendly. Relaxed. But when we got there that night he acted the way he had the first time he saw me, quiet and watching, intent, as if he was still saying, Tell me what to do. I wanted to talk but was afraid I'd say something stupid so I said I loved classical music but didn't know anything about it because I never listened to any until I came to Berkeley. *Why not?* I couldn't say. I could have told him about my father sitting in front of the television all night, and my mother taking college courses but keeping all her books out of sight, sitting with my father and laughing an awful, hollow scraping laugh each time he laughed. Or I could have said all my friends listened to rock music, expecting him to remember how when you're in high school you want to be like everyone else, but I knew he must not ever have been that way, wanting only to be like everyone else. I didn't think he'd understand how I had longed to shrink short and delicate and blonde and how at the same time I prayed and prayed every night to a god I thought looked a little like the old Japanese man down the street, to take me out of San Jose where I was the wrong size and thought the wrong thoughts, and put me on a magic carpet and fly me to . . . to someplace else where I really belonged. When I found myself really saying all these things to Ken, I stopped, but he didn't laugh or back off from me the way he had been doing. *I'm glad you couldn't shrink short. Now I won't let you.* Saying that must have scared him because then he did start to back off and talk about finding our seats when all at once this sweet, low, wobbly voice came warbling, *Ken? Kenneth Franklin, is it you? How long has it been? At least two years since I saw you at Cody's. I've been in the store again and again but never found you. Aren't you working there anymore?* That was when I found out that he worked part-time in one of the bookstores on Telegraph Avenue. His voice had been easy and warm when he started talking to her, but it got tight again. *Yes, I'm still there.* As if he thought she would disapprove, though she didn't seem to, just happy to see him, happy to meet me. *Ceylon! What a splendid name!* She told me about herself in a quick summing up to smooth Ken's silence, how she had retired from teaching ten years ago and bought a house in Mendocino, but *truth to tell...* Maggie always uses quaint little phrases like that, saying them like she's putting quotation marks around them, putting on what Ken calls the little-old-lady act she invented back in the fifties to tease the FBI agents who hounded her. *Truth to tell, I haven't had time to retire so I keep an apartment here and what with nieces in San Diego and nephews in Vancouver I fly like a migratory bird north and south. But while I'm here I want you to visit me.* Then she took my hand in both of hers, such tiny little bird claw hands that she needed both of them to hold one of mine, and her warm, shaky voice sounded like deep red wine pouring into a goblet. *My dear, he was the most brilliant student I ever had!* Ken grabbed my arm and mumbled something about getting seated. *But you must come to tea. Promise.* I felt Ken hesitating, then loosening, then throwing an arm wide around her, hugging her and making her laughter tremble as if to show he forgave her for calling him brilliant. He loved her as much as she loved him. I could tell by the way he talked about her while we were waiting for the music to start. She had been his teacher in high school, twenty years ago. *A teacher like none I'd ever had. She was in Spain during the civil war, in Paris till just before Hitler came in. She worked on a communist newspaper and her lover was an artist who was arrested and died in a concentration camp. But she got out, came back home and got a teaching job in New York, lost it when someone called her communist, went to Hollywood and wrote for the movies till she was blacklisted, finally ended up in a little private school in San Francisco that paid so poorly they didn't ask too many questions. My school. Best teacher I ever had.* I asked why he never saw her anymore, and that made him tighten up again and mutter something about being a great disappointment to her, and I could tell from the sound of his voice that if I asked any more questions he would...but the conductor came out just then and everyone clapped, then rustled, then hushed to unmoving quiet, and into that stillness came a tiny breath of sound, like a dream, so soft I wasn't sure I was hearing it until it grew and swelled, taking me up like wind. That was the first time I heard PSYCHE and it wasn't until later that Ken read me the story of the girl...Psyche...soul...swept away and loved by Love himself, who forbade her to see him but she looked and lost him and had to do impossible tasks, finally going all the way to Hades and back before the gods let her belong to Love forever. Even though I didn't know the story that night, something in me heard it all in the music, heard more because the music tells something deeper than the story, as music always says more than words, and all of it came into me because I let it, let it make the decision for me after we left the concert hall and walked down the street below Telegraph and ended up standing in front of Ken's place, where he gripped my shoulders and shook me, furious, while I reached out to touch his face, feeling his dry, hollow cheeks, his taut jaw under the wiry, close beard as he shook his head. *All to end in bed again? Sex. God, I'm sick of it. Don't we know any other motions? You're young, Lon, don't let me take you through the old, tired patterns again. Or, anyway, if you must, go through them fast, get rid of me, quick, before. . .you're not listening.* No, I wasn't. I only took his hand and followed him down the narrow alley, then down the steps to the door that stuck and creaked but finally opened into the old, moldy-smelling room with hardly space for anything but a bed where that night our baby was conceived. Where I knew Ken, knew all the main lines of him there, his gentleness and goodness, knew it all, and from now on it's just filling in the details. *No, no, you don't know me. You don't know me at all because if you really saw what I am it would be all over, all. . .my God, you're a virgin.* So I told him I wasn't so pure, it was only that giant women weren't much in demand in San Jose. *I didn't want to hurt you.* But when I said he hadn't hurt me at all, he just talked on and on until I knew he meant more. He said that when I knew him I wouldn't want him. *In any case, I'll leave you because I'm not to be counted on, I've made a life out of non-commitment. People like me don't love.* But everything in him loved. The way he held onto me, wanted me just the way I was, but not pressing anything on me, not using, just touching and being touched and giving. Giving himself so simply, contradicting everything he was saying, fitting himself to me, letting me feel as strong as I could ever be, making me free, unafraid, sure that I was strong enough to hold him without lies and hurts. So I did, holding and squeezing him into myself, gripping him with my deepest inner muscles, with strength I didn't know I had, holding and moving, making the rhythm he gave himself into, pressing him into me until my strength crushed, burst, dissolved him through me, into my blood, streaking out to all the edges of my body, to the tips of every hair, and then out, out into the darkness around us. I felt his tears on my cheek, but I was too surprised to cry or even to speak, afraid to make the sound that would cut the darkness before I knew what had happened, how and why I had changed. Because I had, I was different. I knew another part of myself that I hadn't known before. The part that holds on. Though it didn't look as if I could hold Ken. He disappeared the next day, stayed away, trying never to come back to me, though it was already too late. I was in his life now and no matter how afraid he was, he would have to make room for me. Because it was time, because the change for him had come and I was part of it just as he was part of my change and neither of us could run away from

There. Again. Faint, but rising like a stomach ache starting, but fading as soon as I start to pay attention, to think about it. Fading into a little shiver, a cold stab. Of fear? No. What time is it? Maybe I should be keeping track of them just in case this really is—but I took my watch off to do the dishes. There. Right over the sink on the little shelf Ken made. Feels like about 9:30. Can't get the minutes in between on this watch, too small, and I didn't want to spend more money on a bigger one. If I'm timing pains I don't have to count right down to the second. The doctor said ten minutes apart, even five, would give us plenty of time to get to the hospital even at night when we have to go slow. How long? Seemed like more than ten minutes. Next time I get one, if I get one, if that's what I'm getting, I'll time it and in the meantime I can pack my hospital suitcase. That means I'll have to unpack so I can pack. All the stuff packed up, mixed up together to go to Maggie's Mendocino house where I thought we'd have plenty of time to sort things out, pack my hospital things, since I don't need much and it's all stuff I can easily feel, like the robe and slippers and nightgown, not like cotton shirts that I get mixed up and have to ask Ken what color I'm wearing. I'll get the hospital things into this small case so that when Ken gets back we can—fumbling, what's wrong with the catch? Nothing. It's my fingers. Shaking. Afraid? No. Yes. Scared and glad. Scared to have the baby but glad to get it over with, to get it out of my body. My body. It doesn't feel like my body anymore. Taken over, moved into, turned into a rubber doll body stretched over the real live thing growing inside, everything in my body crowded out of the way and my skin all stretched out ready to burst like a balloon. I've been crowded out, out to the edges of my own body, and I can't believe I'll ever be let back in to the center. Mom said after a woman has a baby her body never really goes back to the way it was. I forgot, wanted to forget because that was just another way she had of saying she never wanted to have children but I guess forgotten things don't vanish, just wait their turn to come back when you're not looking, when you're too tired or scared to—scared? No! Just a little. Mom was right. Even if my body goes back exactly the way it was, my mind won't. I won't forget the feeling of these last two months, of my body not being mine anymore, going tired or dizzy or stupid, dropping things or just deciding to cry and not paying any attention when I ask why I'm crying because it's too busy with this big job to bother with me. Me? But there is no Me separate from my body—well, now there is and I wonder if I'll ever feel the way I did before. How was that? Can't even remember. To be flat in front, to roll over on my stomach and sleep, to bend and reach and move without worrying about straining or falling. But even before I was pregnant I worried about falling. Not like Evelyn, who counted up her bruises like medals and said anyone who wasn't getting bumped wasn't doing anything. She wasn't afraid of anything, or was she? *Baby, it's what scares you, you got to do,* she'd say in that rough black accent she put on and took off whenever she felt like it. Her favorite story was how she broke her nose *on the bow of a boat in the middle of University Avenue!* She was crossing the street and her cane slid under a parked trailer carrying a boat, and she went head on into it, knocked out, her nose broken. That's what's scary about cane travel. There could be something jutting out above where the cane reaches and you crash right into it. Head-on. It happens to everyone and Evelyn's right, you have to make yourself not care or you'll never go anywhere. Like me. That's why they switched people around and gave me Evelyn for a roomate. So I could learn bravery, catch it like a cold. I wanted to catch it. I wanted to be like Evelyn or even like Eddie who wasn't really brave but just tough and mean. Those were the people at The Center I noticed, who were solid and real to me even if I was too shy to make friends with them or with anyone else until Evelyn decided to make me her friend. And though I never got to be like her, I did catch a little of her nerve just from listening to her, hearing the way she would come down the hall late at night. I could always tell it was Evelyn by her boots. Not like my boots, not farmer's wife boots, but slick, knee-high laced boots with taps on the soles and heels, a dozen pairs of them, all different colors. Clackety-clickety-clop down the hall with her cane plowing the floor straight in front of her. They never could get her to swing it the way we were supposed to. She held it like a sword she might lift up to stab somebody. That's what she did a couple of times when men bothered her on the street. But she wasn't violent like Eddie, not unless she had to be, unless you call it violent to stab people with words. She was the only person I've ever known who always said exactly what she was thinking, never mean or small, just true. Sometimes hard and hurting, but always honest so it only hurt like touching, locating a sick place, never making the sickness. But her truth got her into trouble with the teachers, especially the blind teachers who she said were like old-style black teachers who tried to make everyone act whiter than white. Calling Mabel Insell *Mrs. Super-blind* because Mabel wanted her to get rid of her boots, and earrings that hung down almost to her shoulders, clinking and jingling when Evelyn tossed her head while she was talking or walking or laughing or just sitting nodding to the rhythm of music playing—or not playing. Once she came in late when I was asleep and came into my dream, a black horse galloping down the hall, clattering its hooves and clinking its bridle, then crashing our door open, tossing back its black head and giving a loud, neighing, *Whoo-ee!* That was the night she broke up with Theodore, one of the partials who was after her, while everyone else was after them because they were like movie stars in a bunch of ordinary people, as if having a little sight made them handsome, talented, kings like the one-eyed man in the country of the blind. *God damn!* That's all she said, over and over as she pulled off her boots and threw them across the room. She always had trouble finding her things, but she couldn't stop herself from throwing them around when she got mad. It did her good, she said, and was worth it even if she had to crawl and feel around the next morning to find things. I noticed that she usually threw things toward one corner where they'd be easy to find after she cooled off. *That smart-ass, fat-head, one-eyed moron! Can't see nothing, never will. Every total around here sees more in five minutes than he's ever going to see in his whole life. And I wasted a month on him. Enough to make you throw up. Learn a lesson. Yes, I did, I learned a lesson from that one. Write that lesson in red all up and down my body. No, in Braille, honey, in Braille, punching them holes up my legs and arms to make sure I don't forget.* By that time she was sitting on the edge of my bed, laughing so hard the bed rocked and wiggled, shaking her clinking head, whispering a long *shi-i-it* whenever she stopped for breath, quieting down so I could ask her what happened. *We went out to the Blue Pony again. Seem like we spent every night there for two weeks, when we weren't up in his room.* Or in ours. Almost every afternoon before dinner when I came to the room, the signal was out, the rubber band looped on the door knob, keep out, private. *And some guy came in that he knew and they started talking. I'm sitting there sipping my drink and listening. And listening. Once or twice I say something, but they just wait till I'm through and then go on where they left off, you know how men do. Talking about sharp deals, and how this guy could use Theodore in his business, selling door to door, magazine subscriptions and cheap records and some kind of phony furnace inspection, and about six other rackets. He like to get handicapped salesmen because it was harder for people to refuse. Then he finally turns to me and says he could use me too, in West Oakland or even in the black part of South Berkeley, though they didn't fall for the pitch as much as the poor people in West Oakland did. Then Theodore starts telling me how great I'd be, until all at once, finally, the light goes on in my head. I been going to bed with this guy, then sitting and listening while he talks this racist garbage, makes his plans for how I can cheat my people. Not only that, once I start to think about it, I can't find one thing we agree on, one thing we can talk about. And he's not that good in bed. I don't even like him. All he has is partial sight, nothing but partial sight. And I was trading my body and my time. Selling it to this stupid, red-neck, crooked—I got up so fast I knocked my chair over and my knees came up under the table, tipping it so a full pitcher of beer fell into his lap! I do feel good about that! And while he's jumping up and yelling, I've already grabbed my cane. But he had led me in, me not paying attention, so I didn't know how to get out. So I started crashing into chairs and tables, too mad to stop and think and figure it out, and someone said I was blind drunk and they were going to call the police, so I yelled just show me the door and you'll never see me again! Not him, not Theodore, I wouldn't let him touch me. Still could hear him yelling, she's crazy, when I was already out the door. Took me half an hour to get back here, going in circles, too mad to ask anyone, too mad even to hear if there was people on the street till I got up to College Avenue and some girl pointed me in the right direction.* She grunted. The bed stopped shaking. *Everybody around here looking for a partial, sell themselves body and soul for a partial. Well, not this girl, no more. I got no time left for people I hate.* I thought she meant her time at the Homer Center was almost up, but later I knew that must have been the day she began to realize she didn't have much time left anywhere, though that didn't stop her from doing it again and again, *Buying myself a sighted man,* then getting disgusted with him and herself, kicking him out, later on picking them up all over the world and signing those postcards Evie and Juan, then Evie and Yuri, then Evie and—but that night in our room she was in her never-again stage and so mad that a few minutes later she punched Louie the Lurker, who might have been more than one man. We never figured out for sure who it was who came down from the men's floor in the middle of the night a few times a week and stood outside our door. We could hear him breathing out there, and after a while Evelyn would yell *Go away, go away* until finally he would go. She named him Louie the Lurker and said he was madly in love with me, to make me laugh, because hearing him out there made us both nervous. But that night, after she got into bed, we started to hear the breathing outside the door and this time she jumped up and ran to the door, yelling at him to go away, then pulled the door open, punched out with her fist and hit him in the eye. He didn't move so she punched again and that time she hurt him. I heard him give a little whimper before he moved away, a whimper like the crying we heard at night. Someone was always crying at night, and when it came down through the ceiling, from the men's floor, it was the worst. Sometimes mixed voices crying came through the ventilating system, different sounds from anyone's daytime voice so the nights were haunted by ghosts crying, ghosts of people who in daylight were always cheerful because that's the way we were at the Homer Center. That was the unwritten rule, be cheerful because being blind was a little problem we solved by learning cane travel and Braille and abacus, but otherwise we were just like everyone else (finally was I going to become just like everyone else?) only better, because there was that long list of famous handicapped people that Mr. Canfield had learned by heart and recited over and over and there was the list he said we should all make, a list of the advantages of being blind, the things we'd learned from

Starting? Creeping through me. Seeping. No, rolling softly up and over. . . time? Ten, twelve minutes since the last one? A long way to go. We might just stay here all night and then drive to the hospital in the morning. No, Ken will say we have to get there soon just in case things speed up. But I'll light the fire anyway because we'll have plenty of time to sit by it together and talk about the weekend and the baby and all our plans to make our life and the baby's life better than either of us hoped we—ah, warm, that feels good. We'll sit and list all the work we have to do, all the hard, good projects Ken has stretched ahead of us for years and years. . . the way Mr. Canfield used to list all the advantages of being blind. *The higher challenges, the deeper victories* and *all that crap!* Evelyn said each time she mimicked the talk he gave in his office to each entering student. But he was a nice old man, and the Homer Center was the prize of his whole life's work, and he knew every student by mass and sound within a week after they came and was like a father to everyone, even to the ones who were older than he was. And it was probably good for most people to be told over and over that being blind didn't change anything, probably made them feel better, not worse, the way I felt when I heard him say it, because I'd always hoped for change. *List the advantages of being blind.* So I told him how I felt relieved because there were so many things I wouldn't have to bother with. What I meant was that I wouldn't have to worry about being too tall to get a man or about being smart enough to get some job besides typing or about other things I didn't get a chance to say because Mr. Canfield got very upset and put his arm around me and said I mustn't think that way, mustn't give up. *I'm not going to let you use your blindness as an excuse to withdraw and give up on life.* Then he told me how he went to college and taught school and lobbied in Sacramento for blind rights and for money to start the Homer Center. *You're not a giver-upper, are you?* Then he gave me a squeeze and left me. He was right, I had given up, had sat around the house for almost two years and even when I got to the Homer Center I learned so slowly, partly because I was afraid to try, so how can Ken say I'm brave and strong? But being afraid wasn't all. There was something more, something good about going blind, words Mr. Canfield wouldn't let me say and try to hear what they meant, so I never had a chance to think them through. Not until Ken and I came here where I have time and space to think and understand the feeling I had right after I knew I would never see and be like other people. Freedom. From a lot of things that just didn't matter anymore. Things that seemed to make up just about everything in my life but that were like a great clutter of stuff spread over the real things underneath, getting between me and what was real. All my life, from the very start, these little things had been piling up, more and more of them every year, like a lot of gadgets you can't use or clothes that don't fit or games you don't want to play but must because that's what people do! Going blind was like a clean sweep brushing away all the Things People Do, so that I could get down underneath all that and stand on a bare, hard, solid place that had always been there, real but forgotten, covered over. And even while I stood still there, trying to remember, to feel the solid place again, even though I was helpless too, and quiet, I was starting... starting...but Mom only saw the helpless part and tried to help by sending me to the Homer Center where I wouldn't be allowed to be quiet and stay inside myself, so far in that I couldn't come out again. Would I have stayed in? I don't know. Maybe I could have got stuck inside if she hadn't sent me to The Center. But Mr. Canfield was wrong to call that time at home *wasted in self-pity.* That time wasn't wasted. It was spent dropping things because I had to lose everything before I'd be ready to go out and find a place where I could belong. That place wasn't San Jose and it wasn't the Homer Center. I learned important, practical things there, but I had to hold out all the time, fight to hold on to the part of me that I had found again because finding it looked to everyone, everywhere, like despair, like dying. Except to Ken who sees something solid in me, solid but unformed. What a funny thought, impossible, solid but unformed! Words only mix things up so I stopped trying to explain my search for that part of me, even to Ken. People who love each other don't have to understand everything about each other. Can't. I can't understand Ken's fear no matter how Maggie tries to explain. *Fear of...yes, of success, of commitment. Of course, Ceylon, you don't understand. You grew up in a different time, even a different place than Ken. Yes, this whole country is a different place, truth to tell. And you know, my dear, if some of the differences are good, and I'm sure a few of them are because you came out of them, well, people like Ken helped create some of those good differences. By his sacrifice. By refusing success when it was offered to him. Oh, sacrifices like his don't turn the world around. I've lived long enough to know that. I suppose they just keep some worse things from happening, so a lot of the bad goes on and on, but somehow... we go on too.* I didn't understand a word she said, but I understand what it means to be afraid so I can feel Ken's fears even if I haven't experienced what he has. I don't believe you can't understand something unless you live it, all of it. No, if you have imagination, something in you is living some part of what everyone lives. So if I live long enough and think hard enough, some day I'll understand why Ken runs away from what he wants. Or used to, the way he was always running away from me. Like that night after the concert when we made love and we were so close and then I didn't hear from him for two weeks. He stayed drunk for two days, then kept away from Telegraph Avenue and campus where he knew I'd look, then started watching me pass on the street and even followed but never let me know he was near. While Evelyn was telling me to forget him. *Get a checkup for the clap and forget him. He's one of those guys who gets off on blind women. Sure, lots of them, can't make it with a normal woman, too scared, so they go after a blind woman, just like some of those black dudes used to go after the mousy little white girls who'd never talk back to them like a black woman. Makes them feel strong for once. Ask any blind woman. Just remember, girl, learn, so the next time you run into one like him* and the next day I did run into him on Telegraph and he let me, gave in and finally let me touch him again. I knew when my cane touched his shoe and he just stood there facing me, not backing off the way people always did, making me feel I could part the waves with my cane, sweeping everyone to the sides where they stood and watched me without seeing me and pitied me without caring. No, he stood there, a tight, hard shadow, while I decided to wait, just as hard, wait and make him speak first. *Still wearing your work boots*. Yes, I told him, they were almost broken in, almost ready for . . . and without meaning to I told him my dream, my vision of myself in boots, outdoors on a hill, climbing, someone holding my hand. Then he took my hand and sighed as if he was tired, but again I waited until he finally spoke again. *Cup of coffee? We're right in front of the Med.* The Med? *The Mediteraneum. A coffee house. A hangout. If you've never been in the Med, it's time. Come.* And he led me into a steamy, smoky—cave deep in the earth with a high, roofless top disappearing in shadows where echoes and hot breath rise and hang. Echoes of tides of sounds swelling and shrinking. Sad laughs and angry moans and fast, harsh words grating on each other. Hot and clammy, near the center of the earth where restless spirits wait for the day of their rebirth, not wanting to be born, afraid to try again, tired of their past lives but still full of them, telling them and asking each other, is it worth the trouble to try again? Can I have a little more time to decide? Bones clattering in shivers of fear. Sharp hisses of serpents? No, bursts of steam from cracks in the earth? Past lives grating and scraping as they are dragged back toward the darker corners of this place where Psyche went searching for—but I didn't know her story yet. It was later that Ken read it to me and I said Hades sounded like the Med and he laughed and said it was. I sat down while he went to get our coffee. *So they put her in Herrick Psychiatric and I couldn't leave the house for two days because she had cut my clothes up into little pieces, even my shorts, everything.* That was the first voice I ever brought out of a crowd, and the Med was where I learned to pick a sound and focus on it and bring it out of the noise. The only sound I could never catch at the Med was footsteps, so that voices and bodies glided up to me and then floated away again. It's easier here to pick sound out of wide places that never squeeze sounds together that way. But I learned it first at the Med where voices glided or dove onto our table, greeted Ken, shook my hand, then crowded in talking all at once as if going on with an argument they'd started long ago, while I aimed at the voices around our table, separating them from the hissing roar around us, sorting them out. A black man reading from his novel of the sixties which he was writing at the post office where he worked. A high-voiced, breathy, sad woman interrupting him. *I'm sick of everyone's lousy novel of the sixties. I'll read you a good poem!* A man who mumbled a few words that sounded like German, then laughed, then mumbled again, laughed. And over them all a voice with a different pace, fast, furious words, New York accent, words that wanted to sweep them all away but only crackled through them. *This California . . . these dry bloody hills . . . this drying up . . . my life!* But I forgot them as I felt the tension growing in Ken, his silence wrapping and twisting up and over and over us like a string wound tighter and tighter on a ball that is suddenly dropped and rolls away, unraveling, Ken jumping up, scraping, pushing to get away, grabbing my arm hard, hurting as he pushed and pulled me as if we were escaping from a fire. *So long, Bye Ken, See you*, rising through the murky roar, Ken saying nothing, answering nothing. Outside, I loosened his fingers from my arm, then took his arm but didn't try to say anything, didn't try to break into his anger to ask why. I waited till we reached the corner, waited for the light to change, then crossed the street. Finally I asked him what was wrong. His face was turned away from me so I could hear only half of what he said. *Shouldn't have taken you . . . same old . . . sick of . . . never change . . . boring.* I told him I wasn't bored and I thought his friends were very interesting, but that was the wrong thing to say. He stopped and turned to face me. *Local color? Interesting characters on Telegraph Avenue? Part of every girl's experience. Right. But just one look is enough. Don't hang out with the local color. Faded color, faded old boring leftover stupid local color. Understand? That's not for you!* His voice got softer and tighter, but I felt him screaming from some deep place. *Waste. Don't waste your time, Lon. Don't waste your time with someone like me. Understand?* I shook my head and we just stood there facing each other like fighters waiting to see who would punch first and then he did what he thought would convince me faster than words, turned and left me, walked away and left me on the avenue. And that was when some sick-smelling stoned kid threw his arm over my shoulder, hissing *acid? grass?* and I swung out my arm and knocked him down while laughs and cheers rose up from the gutter, from the squatting shadows who usually only moaned *change. . .change* and their laughs were angry, like Ken. I wonder how many times after that he warned me not to count on him, that he'd always be running away or letting me down. But he never has, except for the little times, like after our wedding when he got drunk and passed out and I saw him at his worst, just as well to get the worst over with. And after we signed the papers for this place and he disappeared and came back the next morning hung over. It's when he's on the edge, on the brink of getting or being what he wants, something that had tightened and tightened . . . snaps, and he runs away, blacks out, panics. I told him, never mind, no hurt, doesn't matter. *But what if some day you need me and I'm not there? Then what?* I don't know. I guess I'd

It's really just a tiny spot of pain, growing, spreading, swelling to—there. Shrinking? Still there? Fading so slowly I'm not sure when it starts to hurt and when it stops. Must be really happening, has been happening all day. Gas pains! So I've been in labor since before dinner. IN LABOR. Sounds so important, much more important than these little aches. Can't wait to tell Ken. There! There he is. He's coming, scraped the jeep again on the narrow turn just before the clearing. I'll go out and meet him. Put on something warm, the down jacket Maggie gave me for a wedding present. *Warm clothes and books, my dears, the necessities for contentment.* Won't bother with the flashlight. I can lead Ken up the path in the dark. I zigzag up and down faster than he can in full daylight. No, take it easy. This is no time to trip and fall. Behave like a woman about to give birth. How's that? I don't know, don't feel about to become . . . less pregnant. Cold wind. Cold. Should have brought the flashlight so Ken would see me. No, stand here in the clearing and he'll pick me up in his headlights and he'll jump out and run to me and say, *What's wrong?* Nothing, I'm just having a baby. But I don't hear him anymore. Wind blowing the trees so hard, all that brushing and scraping and rustling is drowning out the sound of the jeep. There, a break in the wind, quiet. No sound. Stillness.

Waiting. Animals and birds and bugs all listening to that silence, all of us waiting for what's going to happen, another rainstorm? The shower was a hint, a warning. Real storm coming. Soon, but not yet, not till tomorrow. I hope. Quiet, but . . . no jeep. No Ken. I must have heard the wind making tricky scraping sounds and thought it was the jeep. Because it's about the time Ken should be back and because I wanted it to be him, can't wait to tell him. Better go inside, keep out of the cold, climb up slowly. Or run? Indian women used to run and that speeded things up. Better not speed things up. Just walking down and up the path doesn't do any harm. Good for me, that's what the book said. One of the books. Ken must have gotten a dozen of them, all stacked up on the shelf over the fireplace next to the ones on how to dig and plant and wire and build. Every book he could find on pregnancy and childbirth, reading all of them to me, studying them as if he were going to have the baby. We would have gone to classes too if they hadn't been so far away. I said no, not a three hour round trip at night after the kind of day he was putting in, up at dawn, hammering and sawing and digging to get the place ready for at least one weekend group before winter, just to see if it could work, if it was possible, because we had to prove it to ourselves, to Ken. He had to know this is real, not perfect but real, not another smoky dream out of the Med. He worked so hard, *accomplished miracles!* Maggie said. Covering the stone floor with wood, unblocking the fireplace, digging a new well, a new outhouse, piping in water from the spring, hooking up butane, screening the window, building shelves. I forget all the things he did that Maggie said she didn't know he could do. *I couldn't.* So he asked people in town and he got books and sat up late with the kerosene lamp when I was already falling asleep in the bed Maggie gave us. And the next day he'd be up before light, starting to do what he'd studied, a different man from the one who first found this place on what was going to be our last day together. No, not a different man, more himself than he had been for years, so that finally I begin to understand what it was Maggie tried to explain to me about Ken when we went to see her, when he gave in again, came back, promised not to run away from me again, then asked me to go with him to visit Maggie, as he'd promised, in her apartment in Berkeley, her tiny little nest up high over traffic's ocean sounds, her nest smelling of nutmeg and hanging plants I grazed my head on. *Out on a limb to tell you about Ken.* After a birdfood lunch—cracker bits and sunflower seeds and plums—she sent Ken to the hardware store to get a new lightswitch and install it in her bedroom. *Ken can do those things too, you know. He has always been able to do anything he sets his mind to. Read a book or write one. Fix a car. Play the violin. Paint a house. Nothing, nothing was beyond him. He must love you very much because I haven't seen him looking this way since . . .* I laughed and said he'd only just stopped running away. She didn't hear. She was going on about what Ken was like when she first knew him. *A golden little boy. At sixteen . . . my word, that was twenty years ago . . . at sixteen he was still small, slight, like a boy of twelve, with golden hair that curled all around his face, a smooth, bright face with such intelligent eyes! His voice had changed but stayed light and clear. His fingers and feet were long, long, so long you could tell that he would soon be tall, that any time he would suddenly shoot up. The other boys had become lumpy and heavy, bumping against one another, their voices and thoughts and feel-*

ings rough and confused and cruel. But they never teased Ken. They had too much respect for him. They knew he was brilliant . . . in everything, my dear, so far beyond them. He always finished his work before anyone else and then sat there reading a book. He used to come to me to talk about books, that's how we came to be friends. He had no one his own age who could talk to him about what he was reading and thinking. But I don't want you to think he was solemn and introverted. Mischief? He was full of mischief. So funny. Very naughty limericks on all the blackboards. Caricatures of the teachers. Practical jokes. Oh, not cruel, never cruel. Let me tell you about one so you'll see. I once made a remark about an apple for the teacher and said that in my whole teaching career no student had ever brought me an apple. Next morning as the first class was starting, I opened my desk drawer and it was full of apples! All the other drawers too and the corner cabinet. They came tumbling out all over the floor, rolling. He must have bought two or three boxes of apples! When I think of it, I still laugh. Munching apples, every class, all day. You see what I mean. Never a joke that hurt anyone, but always that gleam of mischief in his eyes, always ready to make a bit of fun. She sighed. *That's gone, isn't it, that's gone for good. No, no, we mustn't say that. Maybe that will come back too.* Now that I think of it, this weekend it must have come back a little in the way Ken teased the choir director when they were all singing around the fire Saturday night. *Bach motets around the campfire? Beats 'Row, Row your Boat'!* And Ken started singing along in the tenor part but just a little sharp so that most people couldn't hear the difference, but the director knew something was wrong and got more and more upset until finally he caught on and threw a pine cone at Ken and we all laughed and they went on singing so I heard for the first time what a beautiful voice Ken has. *Anything, my dear, he could do anything. But I always thought it would be in mathematics. He was taking math classes at the university when he was only in the ninth grade because he had gone far beyond anything we could do for him. Something mathematical and philosophical, I thought, like Bertrand Russell, because he was so brilliantly beyond what we could teach, yet so warm and caring, loving people. Caring too much.* Maggie sighed, then clicked her tongue and sighed again, saying she didn't think she could make me understand the way things were then. *Different, so different. It was all mapped out for young people like Ken in those days. We knew he would go to a good university, become a mathematician or scientist, do research and teach if he wanted to, part of a well-paid elite. Of course, I didn't approve of elites and I raised a lot of questions. Perhaps it was the fault of people like me that young people started asking even more and deeper ones. Some did anyway, and Ken was one of the first. Questions about how their talents would be used. Questions about Einstein on his death bed, regretting that he'd been born. Questions about ways for a man to do his work without in some way serving the takers, the killers. Well, of course, they were the same questions my generation had asked, but we had given ourselves some easier answers: join the Party, sign a petition, walk a picket line. But Ken couldn't accept such partial answers. Once, when I told him about being blacklisted in Hollywood, not allowed to work, he answered that I had sold out, had written those stupid movies that preached the opposite of everything I believed in, betrayed the masses I wanted to help, that in effect I had helped create the mentality supporting the blacklist. That hurt. He didn't spare me even though he loved me. Perhaps because he loved me. And he never spared himself. Perhaps if he hadn't been so intelligent! No, no easy answers for him. He saw things so clearly, saw his place in them, saw everything going on as usual . . . a little minor agitation on the side while brains like his kept the big machine going. That's what he told me when he came home, dropped out of Harvard in his third year, tall and thin by then, quiet, pale. We went on a couple of peace marches together, but otherwise he had just dropped out, dropped away from everything. I told myself he'd soon go back to school, but the years dragged on and the killing dragged on and more and more young people began to appear on the streets, quiet, drugged, stopped. Just . . . stopped. Our best, some of them, truth to tell, Ceylon, our very best!* Then Maggie started to cry. Quiet and low, with the same trembling warble as her voice. She didn't try to stop. She cried the steady way people do at a funeral, maybe a funeral for a lot of people, certainly not for Ken because she wasn't sad about him anymore. She let all the tears run out before she started to talk again. *Once you ask certain questions, confront certain issues, my dear, there's no turning back. Not for someone like Ken. Most did turn back. But not Ken. He kept to the hard way. That's the central thing in Ken, the ascetic part of him. They called drop-outs like Ken lazy or self-indulgent or crazy, but never what they were: uncompromising, ascetic, self-sacrificing. That's what it was, the sacrifice of some of the best young people of a generation. It was like . . . well, when I was in Europe in the twenties, at art school in Paris, every girl or boy I met had lost a father, a brother, someone close, in the Great War as we called it then. Ken and others like him are casualties of a struggle everyone has forgotten now, or worse, remembers romantically as a time of drug parties and flowers and eccentric clothes, forgetting the struggle behind all that, forgetting what's left: wounded men and women, like amputees after a war, missing a part of their minds, damaged by a decision some had to make, cutting off precious, formative years of their lives by eroding the will with questions, questions, the same old hard questions.* Then she gave herself a little shake and her voice was firm again. *Oh, not Ken's will, my dear, certainly not Ken's will. It was his sturdy will that made it possible for him to do what he did, to make his commitment to . . . to non-commitment. Yes, the hard way, that's Ken, only the hard way is the true way for him. And when he sees another choice, another possibility, another hard and true way, I know he will choose that way. Perhaps he has already chosen.* She reached out and touched my hand. We were sitting across a little low tea table and she had to get up, reach and bend over the tea table to lean her hands on my knees and put her head close to mine to say something very important about Ken and me—but just then he came back in so she never said it and I just thanked her for telling me about Ken, though she didn't have to tell me how brilliant he was. I'd starting sitting inside the round counter at the center of Cody's with him while he worked the night shift and I could tell the way they all came to him with questions about books, books on any subject. And there were those professors from the university who came on Friday night and hung over the counter playing some kind of mathematical game Ken had invented. Laughing. Ken laughing and giving me a hug, asking if I was bored, then squeezing my hand like he never would let go until I had to

Oh.

There it is again. Lower? Deeper. Fuller. Steady. Like a deep rumble of a secret underwater earthquake. Fading. Ten minutes? Maybe I should write them down, how many, how far apart. Braille? No, just in pencil on the shopping list paper so Ken can read it when he comes in. Sit by the fire and write down. Fire at its height, so bright I can almost see it. See something, a glow, a flicker. How much I see and how much more I imagine, I don't know, only know it feels good. My old habit at home and then at the Homer Center, sitting and watching for a spark, a flash like the bright streaks that come when you close your eyes. Sit cross-legged and face the fire like a woman out of some ancient time, sitting by the fire and seeing visions. In those old times I'd have been a shaman and I'd tell my visions, not keep quiet about them the way I did at the Homer Center when I'd sit in front of the fire and people would come around, shy ghosts sliding around me pretending to be real people, faking it with imitation laughs that never sounded like real laughs, that's how you can tell ghosts from real people. The totals would be silent, thinking I was lucky to watch the fire and the partials would be silent, doubting I really could see anything, thinking I was faking it. Everyone was always faking it, pretending to see more than they could. Pretending to be real people instead of ghosts. Learning to do things real people do, like boiling an egg or sewing on a button or like just dressing right, which we were all supposed to learn in Mabel Insell's grooming class. *Sounds like it's for horses*, Evelyn would say. *Sure ain't for people!* But Mabel was very patient and very sure she understood what we needed, reminding us that she had been blind for three years before an operation brought back most of her sight. *So I know what you're going through.* Mabel worked hard on us, trying to make us look right. Harmonizing colors. Neat hair styles. But nobody wanted to look the way she wanted us to. Everyone wanted to wear what was in style last year: patched jeans, bushy hair. *Sighted people can afford to be sloppy, but a blind man with a missing button is considered too helpless, pitiful.* What about Evelyn with her purple eye make-up, bike-chain earrings and orange knee boots? *Evelyn, blind women can't afford to look too eccentric. Because there's so much prejudice against the handicapped.* I knew Mabel was right about the prejudice because I remembered when I was in high school, that boy in the wheel chair. He wore a vest covered with badges, an Indian band around his head, and on warm days, shorts that showed his withered legs, bright tassels streaming from his wheelchair. I thought he was awful, that he shouldn't be silly and conspicuous. I wished he wouldn't advertise...I'm getting all hot thinking about that, blushing, ashamed. Just because he was crippled, I thought he didn't have the right to dress in the latest fad, to be silly, to have fun like everyone else. I guess I wanted him to feel ashamed, hide, be quiet, let us forget him, instead of making us notice him. That's terrible, but it's the way most people feel, and Mabel was just trying to get us to adjust to it. *Some things I'm not about to adjust to and it ain't your business to make me!* So Mabel threw Evelyn out of the class, which is what she wanted so she put in more time in the wood shop. Mabel didn't throw me out, but she finally gave up on me. She thought I put myself together with all the wrong colors because I couldn't imagine how I looked. But that wasn't it. Ever since I was twelve and shot up to six feet, ever since I became a giant girl, I had tried it her way. I let my mother take me to the big woman's store, and I never wore vertical stripes or high heels or all one color or gaudy prints. I learned I had to cut myself in half at the middle, one color above, one below, to look shorter, and that I must never wear—but after the car accident, after I went blind, I gave up all that. Did vertical stripes matter anymore? Did anything? So I started putting together prints against stripes, purple against red. Then odd things, *your scrappy clothes*, Mom said. Long skirts that didn't reach my ankles, men's shirts with good wide shoulders and long sleeves, or long smocks with no sleeves, and a cape. And scarves, around my neck, my waist, my head, all colors that made Mabel Insell groan but made Maggie clap her hands. *How Jacques would have loved to paint you!* Then there was the problem of my hair that Mom said I must have gotten from her redhead Jewish grandfather. I always just brushed it out and tied it down with a scarf which worked pretty well, even though it came twisting and curling out from under. *Really, Ceylon, don't you think* . . . . So I let Mabel cut it and set it and roll it and pin it. But a few minutes after she was done, it started springing up, frizzing out as usual, so she gave up on my hair except to try to stop me from tying it down with a purple scarf. But when I showed up in my work boots, that finished Mabel. *Where did you get* . . . but her voice died off and she sighed and whispered that she had failed me, meaning I was a failure though she never held it against me. She even made my wedding dress just the way I wanted it after trying harder than anyone else to talk me out of marrying Ken. *I've seen him, Ceylon, for years on Telegraph Avenue. He has always been there and always will be. There are many men like him. Always with a woman, a young woman about twenty. The men get older but always have a new twenty-year-old woman. Men like Ken are almost an institution around the campus, the avenue, perhaps part of a girl's development. But only that, Ceylon, only part of the experience of growing up.* She meant well. Everyone at The Center meant well even when they made you feel bad. The blind teachers tried the hardest. The super-blinds, Evelyn called them, always nagging about the generosity of the tax-payer and how we had to prove it justified. Always cheerful, teaching us their hollow ghost-laugh, so that I started feeling we were all ghosts in an old haunted house in those first stories I heard on tape, stories by Poe, read in spooky English voices, and always set in a big old house like the Homer Center, where all the stairs creaked and the bushes scraped against the walls as they crept around looking for a way in the windows, and the eucalyptus tree groaned outside where, someone said, there used to be two trees but one fell over without any warning, barely missing Mabel Insell. Most of the windows rattled as if they would break but were so stuck we could hardly open them except for the ones in the dining room that swung out like doors onto the courtyard. And none of the doors closed right, but always started slowly moving as if being opened by invisible spirits, and we were just more of those spirits, invisible to each other too. But when Mr. Canfield talked about raising money to tear down the house and build a *modern facility*, Evelyn groaned. *Yeah, like the tombs across the court?* She was right. The new dormitory building where we slept was like a tomb, concrete, little square rooms lined up, identical, so you had to feel the number on the door to be sure which was your room, tombs where we ghosts slept between hauntings. *No worse than dorms in any college, but I like the old house, old haunted house, and I'm no ghost. If you feel like a ghost, you get out, you hit the streets with me and you won't be invisible anymore, you'll see. Come on!* I said I'd never been on a picket line or in any kind of demonstration. *Well, about time you did it then.* So we took a few other blind people and went to walk the crips' picket line. *This picket line don't march, it rolls!* Wheelchairs rolled back and forth in front of the movie house while we walked along, sometimes pushing a chair with the person in the chair guiding, giving directions, how far to go, turn around, go back, keep a straight line. I carried a sign WE DEMAND A WHEELCHAIR SECTION and Evelyn handed leaflets to people walking by and got most of them talking to her and agreeing that public buildings ought to make better arrangements for handicapped people. Then she started teaching us protest songs, easy ones that we could catch on to right away. . . we're going to turn this place around, we. . . I can't remember it anymore. But I remember the way she came up to me laughing and hugging me. *How about it, Lonnie, you feel visible now?* I was laughing too, and I did feel different. Not ashamed of being big. Not wanting to hide. Oh, I felt scared and silly and embarrassed. But I didn't feel ashamed of being big and blind, and I didn't feel ashamed of stumbling once in a while, and I didn't feel lonely because all the people in the wheelchairs were saying how lucky they were to get an Amazon to carry the sign. *We all vi-si-ble now!* Evelyn made us all chant with her while she led us like a cheer leader and now I wonder how she could do it, how she could give us so much life, when she had so little left. Or was it only time she had so little of, and a whole lifetime of life to

Less than ten minutes? Glad this pain came. Think ache, think pain welling up. I'd rather think about pain than think about Evelyn dying. Don't want to think about dying. *No guts?* True. I don't have the courage she had to face dying, getting braver and braver as death came closer. I'm more like Madeline, just the opposite, with all her poems about dying while she sipped cappuccino with an extra glob of cream and laughed while she was crying and wrote that terribly sad poem to read at our wedding. *Sad? This is the most euphoric crap I've ever written!* She was the first of Ken's friends at the Med to really talk to me when we went back again after that first time and everyone acted as if nothing had happened and Ken hadn't marched out as if he despised them all. I guess they knew no matter what he did he loved them. So Madeline loved me. *Twenty! Impossible! No one could be so young. I love young people, all the wretched pimply students who hang out in this place. I was a student once too, stopped being a student, still hanging out. I can't leave the young. I don't belong . . . out there with all those grown-ups.* Her voice was like a little girl's and that's the way I usually saw her, no matter how much she moaned about her age. All her poems were young, like what I would write if I could write poetry and if I felt very sad and hurt. All the hurts in her poems were fresh, young, sharp hurts, all open and bleeding, not the thoughtabout hurts of older people but the surprised hurt you feel when you're young and you can't understand and that moment of surprised hurt—

like the time Ken ran away and left me on the avenue—stabs so deep, so sudden, so unexpected that it feels like forever and ever in one minute. (*Self-pity!* Davide would say every time she finished a sentence.) I always thought that as people got older and understood more they felt less and hurts didn't come like red hot irons branding FOREVER into your hide. But Madeline said older people only pretended to be calm and wise. *We're all too proud to admit to the same old pain under the wrinkles and fat.* Davide would laugh and say Madeline didn't know what pain was. The sadder she talked the more everyone laughed until she would start to cry. I wanted to comfort her, but Davide said, *This is what she wants.* She would sniff and make a little humming sound and then start scribbling on a piece of paper while Davide whispered to me that she was writing another poem, that she made all of them say mean things so that she could feel sad and be inspired because sitting at the Med feeling sad was the only way she could write. When Madeline finished a poem she would talk about her life in the sixties . . . *when I was your age* . . . passing out flowers on Telegraph Avenue, reciting her poems to other demonstrators at the prison farm, dancing to welcome the dawn in People's Park. *I was really a dancer, you know.* Then her voice would change and get whiny and old, a very old lady, dying slowly in a frilly, puffed up canopy bed. *Self-pity!* Davide would laugh. *In the seexties you were not Lonnie's age, you were thees leftover from the feefties, old, overipe beatneek, like overripe papaya. You are just posing here all thee time hoping someone weel put you een his lousy novel about the seexties.* Then Madeline would spit words at Davide with a voice all sharp and spikey that scared me because suddenly she was the woman who used to be in my nightmares when I had a fever, a long, flat, wavering woman like a ribbon flicking out like a flat whip and moving, waving, curling and uncurling, wavering closer and closer to . . . not to hurt me, but to disgust me, to make the world all around me so ugly that I knew if she flicked and waved and grinned at me any longer something inside me would break and I would begin to bend and curl and become flat like a ribbon. Then Davide would yell at her that her poems were obscene. *Sensual, my pet, s-s-sensual.* Hissing and slamming her hand flat on the table, then starting to cry while everyone went on talking as if nothing had happened. But she would grab my hand and hold it in a hard, sweaty grip, suddenly a monster risen from a deep pool in one of the hissing cracks in the Med floor, grabbing me with a slimy hand, trying to pull me down into her pool of salty tears, filled by all the sad, moaning spirits and monsters like Madeline, not like the creeping, shamed, silent ghosts at the Homer Center but howling in bitter pride. *Leave the girl alone, you old witch! Leesten to thees, Lonnie, I have just completed thees letter.* Madeline called Davide unreal, *a character out of a book by Saul Bellow*, a man who was always writing letters of protest to people he knew or didn't know. He would sit with me and read them aloud, but only when Ken and I were alone at the table because no one else would listen anymore. Letters to the president, to generals, to heads of corporations, to people whose names had appeared in the paper for one reason or another. Letters to his lawyer, telling him to sue someone. He was always suing someone: a corporation that refused to hire him, a college where he was expelled from a class, a professor whose latest book contained ideas stolen from Davide, a magazine which had once printed an article he wrote, censoring part of it.

And doctors. Many doctors whose treatments Davide said had ruined his health. Most of the letters were so complicated that I didn't understand them, but I liked listening to his voice, a gentle and warm voice, deep and rich like a black man but sometimes, not always, with a Spanish accent. In some South American country *wheech must remain secret,* he told me, he had been a Catholic priest, then left the church and came to Berkeley as a foreign student, but lost his student visa when he demonstrated against the government of his country. *Rather than go back and be put een prison and tortured—I weel not tell you, Lonnie, about the torture they do een my country—I got married. She was seexty and dying of cancer. I took care of her to thee end in gratitude for her helping me to stay here. Two years. Then her family came to grab what she left, and threw me out. I deedn't care. Only I cared that they deedn't come while she was seeck. I loved that woman.* Ken said he lived on welfare as mentally disabled. He took pills to stop from hearing voices. Once when he got up from the table and went to the phone to call his lawyer, I asked Ken if what Davide said about himself was true. *Probably some true, some not. I'm not sure Davide knows anymore. Anyway he has suffered—something. He's still under thirty, Lon, and his hair is white.* Then Davide came back from the phone. *Thees lawyer of mine, he ees always too busy to talk to me. That ees why I talk to you, Ceylon, because you don't see the outer man, the crazy man. You see the man I am inside.* Then he told me he was trying to get up the courage to stop taking his pills and let the voices come back again. *They are very frighten, they tell me worse, worse things weel happen to me, to all. Oh, yes, crazy voices. But I am thinking that they sound crazy because I never really leesten, just like nobody leesten to me. Maybe eef I really pay attention and respect to them, I could translate their message. Eet ees that message I have been waiting for, we have all been waiting for. What do you think, Ceylon, should I try it? Do I have the courage?* Ken said people like Davide and Madeline liked to sit near me and talk to me. *You're strong, healthy, normal, yet you can accept them with all their handicaps.* Me! Normal? *Your handicap is superficial. Socially acceptable. It's different with us, with the group that gathers at this table. The ways we've been blinded or wounded go deeper than what happened to your eyes. And are not . . . socially acceptable. You're patient with Madeline and Davide. You understand that they can't help the way they are, anymore than you could help what happened to you.* I told him Davide and Madeline were not only acceptable, they were models at the Med because I'd gotten to know people who hung around our table acting and talking like Davide, crazy and lost and outcast for an hour, then went back to their jobs as teachers or social workers or accountants. And while Ken laughed and laughed and hugged me and said I could see through anything, I was thinking that he had started talking about Davide and *the group that gathers at this table* as if he belonged to it and ended by talking about them as if he were separate. And not jumping up and running away as he did that first time he brought me in there, but quietly, with love, not noticing that he was separating himself from them, just asking for understanding of them, not knowing that in some deep place he was deciding to leave them now, deciding that his wounds and my blindness were not too heavy to carry along while we moved on and found strength in spite of them, maybe partly because of them, strength to try again and

It doesn't hurt that bad. More now. More? Just at the very—top—for a second or two? It's so—going down. How long does it last? Next time I'll count seconds. I'm standing! At attention. As if I could face the pain and talk to it. Argue with it. I don't like you, pain. I don't like the way you sneak up on me—it makes me mad. Don't want to be hurt. Don't like being patient, waiting for Ken. I'd rather argue. Fight. If I had something to fight. Anything, fight, just to do something, like—like Eddie. Haven't thought of him since we left, since long before we left Berkeley. I wonder what happened to him after that day he decided to fight back even if there was no one to fight. That was the day Evelyn told me she was going to die. We were sitting in the courtyard just outside the big glass doors of the dining room, and she was quiet before she started talking fast, telling it all at once. I knew she was diabetic but I didn't understand yet what that meant. *It means first your eyes go and then your kidneys and then—everything. Those doctors are liars. My doctor said I wouldn't go blind. Then, after I went blind, he said my kidneys would be all right, but yesterday he started talking dialysis.* I told her she would live for a long time like my grandmother who had diabetes but died when she was eighty. But Evelyn said that was different. People who got it when they were old might live a long time. *When you're thirty it's something else. I don't have much time, Lonnie, maybe a few months or maybe a year.* Crash! Behind us. As if the house had been cracked wide open by the terrible words Evelyn was saying. A smashing of glass. Then somebody yelling and crying all at the same time with words I couldn't understand, not words, howls, wild animal howls. Then another yell, another crash. Pretty soon more voices were yelling. Then quiet, then that animal yell and another crash and then the other voices weren't yelling anymore, but mumbling and coming closer and closer to us, coming through the dining room, through the glass doors, out into the courtyard where Evelyn and I had stood up and were waiting for them to tell us what was happening. *It's Eddie. Eddie. Standing up there on the stairway swinging his cane around, smashing all the windows, smashing everything, working his way down the stairway. Nobody can get near him.* Crash! *Somebody call Mr. Canfield.* Crash! *Hell, what can he do?* Crash! Then Evelyn gave a little chuckle and told us all to shut up so she could hear. For a while no one said anything. We just stood there huddling in the cold shadows near the dormitory building, afraid to stand on the sunny side near the house where all the glass doors were because the crashes and yells were coming nearer and we knew he was headed for that wall of glass. We heard soft voices, some of the teachers trying to calm him down, slow him down, but after Mabel Insell's voice said *Now, Eddie* and the math teacher's voice said *Listen, man* we heard the biggest crash of all. Someone whispered *There goes the front room picture window* and all of a sudden we all laughed. Then we were like a crowd at a fight or a football game, tense and excited just before an important play as we heard a siren coming closer and closer then choked off right in front of the house and then feet running up the front steps while an old man behind me chanted softly *Come on, boy, hurry up, come on.* I knew he wasn't telling the police to hurry up, he was telling Eddie to hurry, to take a flying run, to smash out the whole wall of glass, all the glass doors, and spray the shattered glass like fireworks all around us. Then we heard a terrible howl and the policemen's voices. *Get him—that side—grab the stick—ow!* Then they had him and he never did get to the glass doors. But before they had him he broke one policeman's nose with his stick and later when people at the Homer Center told the story, they said it a little proudly. *Pretty good aim for a blind man.* And for the rest of that day everyone moved a little more roughly, talked louder, bumped into each other, not like ghosts but like real solid people swinging their canes so they clashed and tangled in each other like swords in a fencing match. The next day things quieted down and some of the teachers started explaining Eddie. *Delinquent kid, you know, barely eighteen. Blinded in a gang fight out in Richmond. Someone shot him in the head. Miracle he lived.* Mabel said he'd been thrown out of school at sixteen. *That type can't fit in, certainly wasn't able to profit from instruction here.* And some of the students said he smoked a lot of dope and the math teacher called him an unstable personality. Then Evelyn said *Sure, just like all the rest of us!* And that ended all the talk right there and made us look at Eddie again, at ourselves. I had always been a little afraid of him. Once when he tried to get me to go to his room, I could feel his mean fury and knew he would rape me if I wasn't so big. And every time he was around, I backed away from the dark feelings that came out of the mumbled words I couldn't understand. *Just like all the rest of us.* After Evelyn said that I saw that all the time Eddie was just crying like Madeline, just writing his letters to the world like Davide. Shuffling in the dark like the rest of us. No different from us. No different from people I had known before I came to Berkeley. Like Dad. *You'll run into a lot of freaks up there in Berkeley.* At first I thought he was right and that Dad and I finally could agree on something. But after Eddie crashed all those windows while we all held our breath rooting for him, I saw how much Eddie was like Dad. Because Dad was furious all the time too. Always feeling mean, blind mean. He wanted to break up every place we were ever in, all those shiny new houses. But he didn't smash things like Eddie. He just ran. He made us all pick up and go again when he started hating the place we were in, when his hate had filled up all the corners of the new house so that he couldn't breathe anymore and had to crash out of that place and find a new one to smear his hate on. Next to the amount of hate in Dad, what were a few broken windows? So when Eddie was gone I could see him as just like the rest of us. No. Not like Evelyn who only seemed rough and thoughtless and said whatever came into her head and wouldn't do what she didn't want to do. But she never smashed things like Eddie or hated like Dad, never smashed things inside herself like some of Ken's friends. I asked her, if what you say is true, if you really are that sick, how can you not be mad, how can you not smash things just like Eddie? She shook her head, jingling her big earrings like wind chimes. *Honey, when you know the situation is serious you don't fool around no more. Most people just haven't figured out it's all for real.* After that she was quieter than she used to be, not depressed but calm and still and paying attention as if she could hear every thought and see every feeling and wanted to gather it all, all up and fill herself. She started coming with me to the Med, sitting at our table and somehow changing the mood of it, so that different people started coming to sit with us, not only accountants in disguise and not just men, who were always after Evelyn. The lute player from Japan, the botany teacher, the bookstore owner, the lady carpenter, people who were on their way somewhere else. All talking with Evelyn, getting close to her the way I always sat near a fireplace to catch sight of a spark or two. She was a bright fire crackling in the middle of the dark cavern and warming it. Even though she ignored Ken and tried to get me to go away with her instead of marrying him. *I'm going to see the world. Got no time for men.* She did go to other parts of the world. But the men were there too. We got the cards. Postcards from Greenland and Yucatan and France. Love, Evie and Axel. Love, Evie and Lorenzo. Love, Evie. Love. Then nothing until last week when that letter came from Mabel, in Braille so that I could read it and know that Evelyn had died on an island off Alaska where

Here it comes. That tightening around my back, then cramp starting at the center and spreading and—count one-two-three-four-five-six-seven-eight-nine-ten-eleven-twelve-thirteen—still rising, getting to the top? Twenty-four, twenty-five, twenty-six, letting go, going down, thirty-five, thirty-six, thirty-seven, almost gone now, hardly feel—gone. Ken. Please. Come. Ken! Please. Don't think about it. He'll be here any minute. Think of how lucky I am, not to be dead like Evelyn, not to be someplace else instead of here on our place, not to be back with Mom and Dad, sitting there again forgetting everything I learned, no place to walk alone unless I could get a ride to the shopping plaza, but that wasn't like Telegraph Avenue. No street musicians, no Med to sit and listen to people talk. No reason to remember how I'd learned to cook, with the freezer always full and Mom afraid I'd burn myself if she wasn't there and she never was, never came home from the college until almost dinner time when she'd get there just before my father because he'd be mad and ugly if she wasn't. So I sat home alone all day just like before but now lost too in another strange house where they'd moved while I was away at the Homer Center. I wasn't surprised. Dad could never stay still in a house for long. When I was little we had to stay in one for six years because the market was slow and he couldn't sell the house we were in. That was when he took up sky-diving, I guess so that he could feel he was moving, escaping, diving out of his life. Usually we moved in circles. San Jose, Santa Clara, San Martin, San Carlos, San Jose again. All those lovely Spanish names I never noticed until Madeline made a poem out of them. *In California we move among the saints.* How did the rest go? San this and Santa that, always changing Santas. But the houses were always the same. He had to have new houses, from one housing tract to another where the houses were lined up all the same as each other, same as the last tract. Always another garden to put in and Dad hated gardening so he put in a volley ball court but the next year dug up the asphalt and planted lawn, then bought a dog who dug up the lawn so he had the dog killed. *Put to sleep.* Mom held and rocked me when I cried that I hated him, the way I'd heard my sisters say it before they left home, hardly ever coming back and when they did they yelled at Dad and sounded just like him. Mom told me she didn't really want the new house because she knew how hard it would be for me to learn it. *But you know your father.* The final reason for everything. And this house was so much bigger than any house we'd ever lived in. Not in a tract but alone on top of a hill with only roads and freeways and sheer drops and no place to walk with a cane. He was so proud of it he took me around describing the bedrooms, the study, the sewing room, the bathrooms, the deck, guest house, pool, so I began to know long before Mom told me that he had taken some of my money for the down payment and was drawing on it every month because there was never enough from his factory job to make the payments. Still, when Ken found me there and I left with him, it wasn't because Dad was using up my money. The reasons I had to get away from there were much deeper, worse, harder to say yet very clear to me when I came home after being away for six months. Lost in that big house and sitting in front of the fireplace all day, even after Mom said no more fires when I was home alone, sitting and trying to listen to music that was drowned out by the roar in that house, the roar we had carried into every house we lived in, the roaring, aching craving to be—somewhere else. Their house, their choice, their decision but never what they really wanted. A place to escape from, a prison. And worst of all, now I was part of the prison. I was the reason for having the house. *A good investment. We'll take care of it for you and when we die you can sell it for plenty.* As if he wouldn't be looking for another house next year. But I didn't know how much I was part of the prison for my mother until she found me vomiting in the bathroom and guessed right away. *Oh, my God, my God!* As if she were pregnant instead of me and saying *pregnant* as if she were saying *dead.* Never hiding her feelings the way she used to with *I didn't plan to have you but naturally a mother loves her children.* No, none of those lies—were they lies? Partly? No, everything was different between us. I wasn't her child who had to be protected. I was a woman. I was pregnant so I was just another trapped woman like her only worse because I had no husband. *Disgraced, ruined, like some little tramp!* Then she laughed and shook her head and hugged me around the waist, pressing her soft body to me, her smell of roses and cloves that meant soothing, wiping away of tears, trying to touch her face to mine but only coming up to my shoulders. *I'm talking crazy. What's the matter with me? It's just...old feelings...old fears. A different generation. You wouldn't know, don't know how it used to be. Sorry, sweetie, I'm sorry. Heaven knows, didn't I ask you if you wanted the pill when you were sixteen? I knew things would be different for your generation, better. I wish you'd been more careful, but we'll just see about an abortion. You're lucky. It's different for you.* With a little edge of bitterness in her voice, resenting that I wouldn't have to suffer the way she did. I wouldn't have to have the baby. I told her I didn't want an abortion, I wanted to have the baby. *I understand how you feel, sweetie.* But I could tell that she didn't really believe me, didn't think I'd stick to that decision. Because she didn't tell Dad. A week went by and she didn't tell him so I knew she was waiting for me to change my mind and have an abortion. Then it would be all over without him knowing, without any big explosion, without him blaming her. He always blamed her for everything even for the car accident that blinded me, saying he never wanted me to go with those kids. Finally got rid of those kids, the few in high school who wanted a shy giant girl around, the few who all at once or little by little stayed away after I went blind. He always said no to everything, then let her beg and wheedle. *All right, do what you want!* Then he could blame her if something went wrong. Blamed her for the settlement. *We should have got double, but that stupid lawyer you picked* . . . and she must have been afraid he'd blame her for sending me to Berkeley where one of those *freaks* could get me pregnant. But it was worse than that. When she saw after a week that I really meant what I said, really meant to have the baby, she was the one who exploded. *You'll have the baby! You? And who is going to have to take care of it? And take care of you? Who? Me! Again, again. All my life. I'll never be free of these children!* And then she told my father and didn't even listen when he yelled at her. She didn't care. She was too miserable. Furious. I had never seen her that way. I thought and then I knew, she is right. She shouldn't have to have another baby in the house. It was my baby, my responsibility. I said I would move out, get an apartment in town and go to the San Jose Center for handicapped, the address was on a list they gave me when I left Berkeley. They would help me find a place to live and show me how to take care of the baby and since I had plenty of money from the insurance settlement—but then all of a sudden Dad got very quiet and Mom fell into a chair and started crying, softly and steadily, melting into her own tears that poured as if they would never stop. That was when I found out that Dad had plans for the rest of the money, some business to invest in so he could quit the factory. *If you really want to have a kid, want to keep it, I won't stop you.* He was talking so carefully to me now, afraid to yell, afraid I would leave and take my money with me. *Be sort of nice having a kid in the house again, big house like this. Your mother can stay home and help you* . . . while Mom just made dull watery drowning sounds and I stood there between them thinking that I was going under too and wondering if

Take a deep breath—hold it—stop—everything. Why? Should I stay still while it grows—grows—grows? No more. Fading—fading. Does it help to hold my breath? No, that was for later, for when I start to push. Can't hold my breath that long anyway. Or should I pant? That was the other book. Can't remember. Everything we read gets all mixed up in my head. Doesn't matter now, makes no difference what I do. Doesn't hurt much anyway. Later at the hospital they'll tell me what to do, how to breathe, when to—but it's getting late. After eleven? Ken's been gone almost four hours. An hour going. An hour talking with Maggie. An hour driving back. Maybe he waited during that shower. Or a flat tire. Or he drove to town for gas. Any minute now he'll drive in and everything's ready so we'll go. Don't worry. Think of pleasant things, let the fire die down and think about—music. Play some music. That was one thing Ken made sure we would have even without electricity even without a phone (no sense putting one in for just a few months. Maybe never. I like being—but Ken says next year with the baby here we'll need a phone) but music is a necessity, the tape recorder with plenty of batteries and all the cassettes marked in Braille. Bach. Debussy. Franck. Vivaldi. Yes. Vivaldi. There. Bright sunny music, rubbing up and down, polishing up the sun or rubbing sticks together to make sparks or jumping, jumping the way I used to when I was little and I would jump for a long time until I forgot time, jumping up and down, thud-thud-thud in a steady, slow driving rhythm that never made me tired but hammered up new energy so that I could have gone on forever out in the sun on the dry grass in the empty lot next door where the earth throbbed under my thudding bare feet and under my clothes I was a naked wild girl bouncing up to touch the sky and then down to touch the earth after hanging between, free and flying between sky and earth. Think of that. Think of happy, beautiful memories to fill the time before Ken comes as he came the other time when I had given up all hope and sat dead in that strange new odorless house with Dad who wanted my money and Mom who wanted none of us but would never leave and would never deny him what he wanted. Captured, tied up, helpless, waiting for us, him and me and my baby, to kill the last bit of herself, what hadn't yet been eaten away by my father and then my sisters and then me. Cannibals. Marooned on a bare, odorless rock, bare survivors of lifewreck starving on that bare place with nothing to do but keep eating each other. Swim away! Jump off and swim—drown? I said I would leave but I was starting to lose my courage, what little courage I had, so little, not enough to do anything or go anywhere. So there we sat, the three of us starving and someone had to be eaten and maybe my mother was right and it should be the baby first instead of Mom always feeding herself to babies. And why shouldn't Dad use the money to get out of the factory? Maybe that was what made him so mean, working all those years in that roaring-speedup-layoff place. And why should I leave them? How could I when I was so stupid and helpless as to get pregnant and make such a mess of things the first time I left home? I had no one but them. Who else loved me? Mom and Dad loved me in their way. All these thoughts creeping closer and closer so that a couple of nights later when we were all three sitting silent in front of the blaring television with them as blind to it as I was while it roared like the dark sea around our dead, bare rock, I was about to tell Mom to call the doctor about the abortion when the doorbell rang, a clanging oriental chime Dad had just bought, a brassy, wavering sound with vibrations that kept dying away slowly in waves. Listening to those vibrations I knew it was Ken at the door. I knew before my mother opened the door, before I heard Ken's voice asking for me. She knew too and Dad knew and we all stood up and I went straight to the sound of Ken's voice, tripping over the footstool Dad was always leaving in a different place, almost falling on Ken, almost knocking us both down, but he held me and sighed. *You ran away.* I don't think Mom and Dad heard him because Dad had started yelling and that was the first Ken knew that we were going to have a baby. I felt him tense when he heard that, felt his hand twitch in mine as a shiver ran through him and later he admitted it was a shiver of fear but it went right through him and out and away. Then joy rushed in, surprised him and stayed. Dad saw it. He saw that knowing about the baby made Ken hold me closer. *He only wants your money. Who the hell wants a blind girl? He wants your money!* I said Ken didn't know about the money but Ken shook his head and said I'd told him long ago about the accident and the insurance company paying ninety thousand. Since Ken wouldn't yell back at him, Dad had to quiet down and become very old fashioned like an old movie asking Ken what his intentions were. Ken turned to me. *Marriage?* I nodded but he added that my parents were right to advise against it. *I'm much older than you and I have no steady work and sometimes I drink too much as I did when you left me and I tried to forget you but I couldn't.* Then he turned to Dad. *You have every reason to believe*

I would spend her money badly. Let her down. My record so far is not encouraging. No answer from Dad. He knew it was all over. There was nothing to argue about, nothing he could say about Ken that hadn't already been said. No way Dad could touch him. Mom started crying but I could hear some relief in her crying. Relief that she would finally be free of children. Then mixed in with the relief was fear of my father. And a deeper fear so strong that I felt it. I knew she was afraid of herself, wondering what bits of herself were left, maybe not enough for her to do anything with. She tried to cover the fears, tried to pretend she was crying for me. *I think you're making a terrible mistake.* But it came out different from what she was pretending. It came out saying, not that marrying Ken was a mistake but that marriage itself was a mistake and that I would be unhappy because a woman had to be unhappy. That was when something else crept into the tone of her voice. I could hear it all, the way I can hear every separate note in a chord of music. A tone of satisfaction, faint but clear, that I would be weighed down with children, that I would be unhappy as I was meant to be as if it comforted her to think I would be, because only a part of her wanted to escape unhappiness while I escaped it and another part wanted to spread out her unhappiness because it, after all, was what she knew, what she was used to, what she couldn't quite give up. It was so ugly, like a bad sentimental song played on a piano out of tune. I couldn't answer her, couldn't say anything. All I could do was to grab the door knob, open the door, pull Ken, leading us both out into the dark without even stopping to take my clothes, quickly before the tide changed, before the dark waters rose up over that bare, odorless rock and covered us all. That's what Ken calls my courage which is really more like blind, dumb fear. I'm not brave and strong... *and growing stronger,* he says when I deny it. I didn't feel strong in Maggie's car that night riding back to Berkeley shaking when I thought of Dad. *Who the hell wants a blind girl!* Shaking while I told Ken he might be sorry he came to rescue me, then being surprised by his funny, squeaked-out laugh. *Lon, I drove down here to let you rescue me!* Then he talked all the way back to Berkeley, saying he knew as soon as I left that everything was different for him, a change had started without his knowing and we had to keep that change going together and make something new, a new life for us and the baby, and the first thing we would have to do would be to get out of Berkeley. Already I think we knew where we

Pain.

Deeper. Deep. Rounding out to—a—hard cramp—a fist squeezing me—there—there—going away. Almost—gone. Where is he? Where is Ken! He should be back by now! Did he say he was going further? Into town for something? I can't remember anything he said about—stores are all closed anyway. Probably he and Maggie sitting there going over the whole weekend. Why shouldn't they? Ken hardly has stopped to sit and talk to anyone since we came up, except that couple up on the ridge, Burt and Marge, and he promised he wouldn't go there again. The past two months he has stopped only to sleep, working so hard, so he has a right to sit in the car by the main road and talk for an hour or two. Three! If he wants to. If Maggie wants to. I can let her have him to herself for a little while, can't I? After all, they don't know Margaret has decided to come early. Maggie will be so pleased when we name the baby after her. If it's a boy I want to name it after Ken. I insist. Yes, Maggie and Ken are celebrating and she has a right to. This weekend meant so much to her, maybe more in a way than it meant to us because our happiness, our success, just our survival stands for something more to her. She tried to tell me at our wedding after three glasses of wine, after hopping around to all Ken's friends from Telegraph and mine at The Center, introducing herself. *I'm Maggie, the best man!* because she and Evelyn were our witnesses and family and parents since mine wouldn't come and Ken's mother lives in New York since his father died and can't fly because of her heart but wrote a thready-pen note saying she hoped whatever we hoped. Maggie working her way around all the guests then ending up near me. *Just to tell you what this means, what you two mean, how many old hopes are riding on you. For truth to tell so much has failed and died in all the years of this century which is about as old as I am. So many casualties to count. And then to see you two rising from the ashes—oh, no! My word, what an awful image!* She giggled and then her voice broke and she grabbed my hand in her two hands and squeezed tighter than I thought she could and after a minute she could talk again in a kind of whisper. *To see you two, determined to love, loving. Accepting, eyes wide open, ignoring all the damage this world has managed to inflict on you both. Transcending it. With such courage. To love and build. Courage to make promises. I didn't think anyone made promises anymore. And you, my dear, wise. Wise beyond anything I imagined. I can't think how you became so wise so young. You've made me determined to live for a very, very long time yet.* Another little giggle. *Just to see it all work out!* Then she apologized and said she was tipsy and rambling and I wouldn't understand a word she said. But I did. She was calling us brave and strong when everyone else thought the same thing as Mom and Dad, that I was foolish, careless, thoughtless, childish—just letting everything happen. Taking Ken's strange arm on the street and hanging on—waiting for him each time he ran away from me—letting him come back—letting myself get pregnant—marrying—putting all the money into this land and moving up here to live—how? Letting all this happen in just a few weeks, not even knowing each other except to know the worst, that I'm a blind girl with $90,000 (minus $28,000 Dad spent) who turned herself and her money over to an old Telegraph Avenue drop-out. That's the way the others saw it, all except Maggie. They all warned me. *Don't marry him. Wait a while. Being pregnant is no reason. You can get an abortion. Wait a while. Live with him a while in Berkeley. See how it goes. Life is too hard in the country. No one can live off the land. Neither of you knows anything about farming. You'll be isolated. It's dangerous. He drinks, you know. Wait and see if he really stops. Don't believe promises. You mean he didn't even promise to stop drinking? Make him promise. Nobody keeps promises. You'll see. You're young, you're not even twenty-one, you don't know what the world is like, what people are like, how good intentions fall apart, how hard it is for people to change, how after marriage people show parts of themselves you didn't know were there, not nice parts, how after the honeymoon is over people can be cruel, when they relax and become their real selves.* Like Mom and Dad. At that dance during World War Two where a slim smooth-faced, laughing marine met the girl with tiny dancing feet and long, soft blonde hair and they fell into each other's arms, strangers in love, letters every day to keep him alive to come back to her. Love winning over death and bringing him back to her. Different. A bully, a restless bully who kept running, dragging her from one place to another while she had two daughters and covered herself in smiles and recipes to hide away from his waves of yelling rage, and from the children she didn't want to have, but when they grew and she went back to school he got her pregnant with me, to keep her, because he was afraid, the brave, laughing marine who changed into a—she told me all that too after she knew I was pregnant, told me so many hard things. I guess she was saying that she and Dad had been young and full of courage once too. For once she wanted me to see her as the girl she had been. But she never told me what went wrong, what made all those brave, beautiful parts of themselves get buried under the weak, mean things, the bad parts that everyone says come out after you're married. Your real selves. Yes! Real. Yes. That's what I was hoping for, what I couldn't explain to all of them because they wouldn't understand, they could only say that I was young and ignorant and was going to be hurt. As if everyone didn't get hurt anyway, some day. As if I hadn't already learned that life hurts. Our real selves. They meant Ken showing his real self. Why must that mean getting worse instead of better? Why does getting married, promising ourselves to each other, have to make us worse? Why shouldn't it make us better, make it easier for us to love? Letting the strong parts out to overcome the weak ones. That's what I had to believe. That there was a big risk in what we did but a bigger risk if we waited. For what? Wait to test Ken? Wait and watch for all the weaknesses we already know about? Wait and watch for an argument, a cruel word, an hour of boredom? Sit at our special table at the Med and breathe that stale steamy air full of warmed-over words? And wait? No. For us, waiting could only hurt, could only drive us apart, which was what everyone else really wanted to see happen, even Evelyn, everyone but Maggie. No. Sometimes you have to jump before you get a chance to think too much. Would we have come here if we had thought about how hard it would be, had asked questions, had really known? Would I have let myself get pregnant if I had thought and read and learned how uncomfortable and sick I'd feel? If we had been cautious, if we had waited, we would have been caught back there, where we were, what we were. Still sitting at the Med waiting for a sign that everything would work out, waiting for a sign that never comes, when what we needed was to get out of Berkeley to try this hard thing and to make it work. They said I didn't know him, but how could I begin to know any but his weak parts if I didn't make an opening for the strong parts of him to come out and to grow. So we had to make the jump, just close our eyes and ears and minds and

Feel it start—growing—spreading. Sharper. Stronger than the last one. Strong! And holding on! Fading. Doctor said five minutes apart, go to the hospital. At the latest. Still more than five? Six? Ken? Oh, Ken, please come. Please. Don't think about it. He'll get here. Don't think. The fire. Fire's dying, think about the fire, build it up. Wood box almost empty. I should fill it, go outside and carry wood from the stack against the side of the house, not too much, just a couple of pieces at a time, easy trips back and forth. Put my jacket on again. Don't get chilled. Slow walking in and out, back and forth. Keep busy. Something useful. So that when we come back in the spring, the box will be full of dry wood for our first fire. Walking is good for me, doesn't hurt, nothing hurts between pains. It's as if there never was a pain. One of those books said there's no pain, just contractions that only hurt if you get tense. But I felt the contractions start, and I wasn't tense. I felt them because they hurt. I guess they hurt worse if I get tense, afraid. I am. Afraid. Less afraid if I keep busy, moving, useful, slowly filling the woodbox. But I know the pains will get worse and worse, and I'm tired of being alone with them. I want to be in the hospital where people know all about this and Ken is with me holding my hand and timing my pains and rubbing my back, the way the books said he should. It'll take us almost three hours to get to the hospital just because of that, because Ken wanted a hospital where he could be with me all the time and the closer hospital won't allow that. So hurry home, Ken, don't make any stops. He wouldn't. No, he wouldn't stop to see Burt and Marge. He never has, not once, not after that first time and he didn't mean to then. They met on the road and Burt hitched a ride and then invited him in to their place. It was right after we signed the papers and moved in. Ken was drawn tight, stiff, in a panic because we'd done it and the responsibility or the hope was too much for him. Otherwise he wouldn't have taken one drink, and if he'd been with anyone else—but Burt and Marge are alcoholics, only my age but real alcoholics, sent up here to live on Burt's family property with a freezer full of food to dry out *in the good clean air with no car and no money* for a year. But somehow they manage to get liquor. Maybe they trade the food for it. They don't say, they only talk all the time about how they want to stop. Broken voices, little old tired voices, but Ken says they look young, younger than I do, just a little pale. *When winter sets in, we'll be stuck out there, then we'll do it. Dry out.* Feeble, whiny voice, so sad I wanted to help Marge, but we couldn't go near them, not after what they did to Ken. *They didn't do anything to me—it was just me.* And they were just there and Ken was in one of his tense times and they gave him a drink and it ended with him passed out for half the night and me sitting here worrying, thinking he'd had an accident. He promised never to go to their place again and he never has, I'm sure. He wouldn't. Wouldn't. Even though by the end of this weekend he was tired beyond rest, tightened up worse than he was after the wedding or after we moved in. Those times when he—dead drunk. I really understood those words when I saw the way he was. Killing his tension, drowning it because something in him tries so hard, gets so wound up so tight that it won't let go. I don't know what it would do to him if he didn't drug it, drown it. *I used to be afraid my mind would crack if I didn't knock it out for a while. But that was before I had you, Lon. Now maybe I can*—though I never told him not to drink. Those times—only three times since we've been together, I never said anything because I see how he hates doing it and doesn't want to and wouldn't if he could help himself. It's a mystery I don't understand so what could I say that would help? I might only make it worse. So I'll never say anything. I'll just love him. Until that tensing up happens less and less until finally it doesn't happen anymore and he won't need to —oh, now that's a fine, full woodbox, and the fire's good and hot. Drops? A few more drops, a quick scatter of rain like rocks on the metal roof. But I love it, the sound. When we had that first rain last week and the roof rattled all night, it only made us laugh. Sometimes it would stop and the wind would stop. Then it would start again very softly, very gently so that the trees caught and held it, then all of a sudden the wind would rush through and shake the trees and they would toss their held rain down all over us again. *Shower of gravel thrown by the hand of the giant who lives down in the valley!* Machine gun fire, we're surrounded! *Meteor fragments sprayed over us from the huge world that just fell deep into the valley, fell with a deep thundering, shaking thud!* The sky is falling! *The sky and the stars.* That first night of rain we woke and played that sleepy game, taking turns naming the noise and making wild pictures to go with it. I had begun to see the pictures in a dream and slid from the dream into waking visions that Ken says he doesn't have, other people don't have. Just me. No, everyone does when they're children. Like when you hear sounds on the radio and imagine the people and places. Once the television picture went out and we had to wait three days for the repair man to come because it was a big set that couldn't be moved. And I sat alone near it with the sound on and listened and imagined what made the sounds, what happened while the music played, what happened during the silences. And everything I imagined was so much bigger and brighter and stranger than anything I saw after the television was fixed—but people laughed when I told, as if they had never seen such things. But everyone sees things when they're little. And then they stop seeing because it's kid stuff and people laugh. I stopped too but when I went blind I let it start again, let the sounds turn themselves into spaces and colors, into scenes like the surrealist paintings Maggie has all over the walls in her Mendocino house, the paintings by her lover in Paris. When Ken described them to me, I knew that Maggie's lover had never stopped seeing things in his mind that way, the way a child does, the way I was doing now that I couldn't see. So I wasn't half crazy since I went blind, the way at first I thought I was, or if I was crazy, other people were crazy that way too and their craziness made beautiful things so they weren't crazy anymore, they were artists getting under what everyone else sees, going right through and into people and things. But Mabel Insell called it *daydreaming! Ceylon, you're letting your mind get lazy and sloppy, the way some blind people stop combing their hair!* Over and over she'd tell me I must concentrate and must not get discouraged and Carol backed her up during cane travel practice. *You must remember the game, deduction, Sherlock Holmes, elementary my dear Watson.* They were right, I had to shut it all out again till I learned not to stumble over things *like a star-gazer who must learn to be a navigator.* But I want to be both. And now that I can do things pretty well and don't trip very often, I can let in all my crazy pictures again. Maggie the bird and Evelyn the horse and the herd of deer running over the rooftop in a rainstorm and Vivaldi scrubbing and polishing the stars with his

Ignore it. Pretend it isn't happening until it reaches—that point where for a few seconds it's—strong—stronger? That must be—there—there! It—lets—go—little by little. Don't think about it. Think about Vivaldi, let go and sink into Vivaldi, slide in between beats and—no, I can't slide in. It's only around me, not in me. I'm too excited, too distracted. Scared? Think about something—something pleasant, a happy scene. The wedding. Our wedding at the Homer Center. Standing up on the table in the sewing room while Mabel Insell put the last few tucks in the dress she made for me, unbleached muslin with insets of rough blue brocade at the breast and full sleeves hanging with lace she had clipped off old pillow cases crocheted fifty years ago by Maggie's mother. Crying and stitching while Maggie and Evelyn laughed at her. Mabel never had said another word against Ken the whole week long while she sewed. It was Evelyn who said *You sure you love him or you just buying yourself a sighted man?* but kept quiet when I didn't answer though I could see that in her own way she disapproved of marriage even more than Mom did. Maggie didn't talk at all, getting so quiet I could almost forget she was there. Maybe she wasn't—maybe she was far off somewhere dreaming about her lover or about some other times like this that were beginnings, full of hope. When she finally spoke, her voice floated up and then down to rest on me like a blue feather. *Beautiful, my dear—like a young goddess. No, no, leave her hair free. Like flame. Like a halo.* She put her tiny hand in mine and Evelyn took the other one and they led me down the big staircase which was wide enough for the three of us. And I walked like a goddess so that everything changed. We weren't on a creaky old staircase in a musty wreck of an old house echoing with hollow laughter and stumbling shuffles of blind ghosts. The old house was restored just as it must have been years ago. Carved mahagony staircase with stained glass windows splashing colored light on every velvet step. Vases filled with lilies, tulips, daffodils. Sunny foyer hung with paintings and mirrors. Bright sun slanting into the window-walled music room where we glided silently across thick oriental rugs to the french windows, tall and broad, opening wide to the old brick-paved court. Plum trees in bloom. Climatis streaming purple. Bright, excited, elegant people talking and laughing and then hushed as I stood in the opening of the central window. Then the cello—Celia playing the same melody she was playing when Ken and I first met. Hands withdrawn from mine, slipping away, then Ken took my right hand. We walked down the two little stone steps to the bricks of the courtyard and stood in the midst of more people than I thought would be there—twenty-four from The Center, Ken's friends from the Med and the bookstore, surrounding us like the music which ended when Madeline began to read a poem she had written especially for the wedding. A long poem about love that started to get sad the way her poems always get, though it didn't make me feel sad because it flowed on and on like the cello music, tone and rhythm, mellow sounds rising and falling. *Hey, can it, Madeline, it's too long!* I thought that would make her cry but it didn't. *Oh, all right, I'll cut this page.* I heard paper crumpling and ripping and everyone laughing. Then she ended the poem with the only line I still remember—*to let old Love nag us back to life.* Then a judge, a friend of Maggie, performed a short legal ceremony before Davide began the special one he had written for us that started off sounding like a Catholic ceremony but then went off into his own words about how our marriage meant something different to everyone there but held all meanings because marriage wasn't ever just a thing between two people. It involved the whole world and everyone in it but in a different way from the way it used to. Then he read off promises for us to repeat, changing them so that we promised to love and honor each other *without forsaking all others.* At the end he said everyone must make vows to honor and support our marriage and to pray for us as well as they knew how and he made the whole crowd say *I do.* A minute later we were walking around being kissed and hugged, lots of wet cheeks touching mine and the music started up, this time Celia with two fiddlers scraping out country music and everyone laughing and dancing and drinking the wine Ken's friends had brought and eating the cake made by the cooking class at The Center. A long, late party and we stayed through the whole thing because everyone wanted to talk to us. They all knew we were going up to Mendocino and maybe, if things worked out, staying up here and they wanted to hear our plans and give advice. *That's what I'd like to do. We may be coming right behind you!* Over and over we heard people say that. So Ken sent all of them a card after we bought this place, telling them we could always use an extra hand and some of them did come in August but none of them stayed more than a couple of days because the work was hard and hot and there was no beer or TV or time to sit in the sun and talk and none of them ever came back. *Never mind, Lon. Some day there'll be people who want to come up and work here and we'll always have room and work and food for them, but I doubt they'll be any of the people at our wedding* who all wished us luck and drifted back to Telegraph while Maggie put the rest of the food and wine into the trunk of her car, handed us the keys and insisted on walking home. *My dears, let me walk off all my feelings or I'll cry again. Be happy, be happy. I'll be up to see you next week.* The last was Evelyn hugging me hard for the last time, not pretending it wasn't the last time, not pretending any hope that we'd be happy because she'd said what she meant and stuck to it—that I didn't really love Ken. I couldn't be sure that she was wrong. I wasn't sure about anything. Love. We had never used the word, Ken and I. That word was all around us in the books and movies and songs and even in the poems. I saw couples together, married people like Mom and Dad or unmarried couples that were together and then not together. But I didn't see anything that matched the movies and poems. And I didn't feel the way the books said, not about Ken. Did that mean Evelyn was right and I didn't love Ken? What did I feel? I couldn't think. It all disappeared as soon as I tried to see it, like those first days when my sight was failing or like Psyche in the story, unloved all her life, then loved by Love Itself but trying to know Love, see Love, holding up the candle to see Love and losing him. I didn't know what my feeling were, if I had any at all, and when Ken unloaded the car at Maggie's house in Mendocino, found the wine and before I knew it had drunk a bottle and passed out, then I understood he must be just as unsure as I was, wondering what he felt for me, wondering if we should have

Oh, fine. That's good. I'd rather time a pain than think about that. I want to think only about good things that—ow—that keep away—fear. All right—enough—go—a-way. There. Good things. Like the week in Maggie's house in Mendocino after Ken said *Well, you've seen the worst now and I can't promise it'll never happen again but I'll try* emptying the other bottles in the sink while I thought we must do something fast, so for the first time I brought out the plan both of us knew we had hidden in our heads since the first time we came up here. We sat close to the pot-bellied stove and talked. And talked. Sometimes I would get up and walk around touching all the tiny sculptures on pedestals, small figures I could hold in my hand, made by Maggie's lover, saved from the Nazis who killed him—the dancer throwing out her arms so wide—the runner with her legs pumping high making me remember when I was a little girl and I ran and ran until pain stabbed my side and my chest and I ran gasping and stumbling until the stabbing left me and I could run easy, easy like floating, could have run forever with the wind pushing the world into a blur rushing past me. Then Ken would walk around describing the paintings on the walls, especially the one of Maggie, the nude over the fireplace, painted when she was my age, a tiny golden spirit like a humming bird whirring in the air beside a flower. Then we would sit down again and talk about our plan, our dream. Then walk out on the cliffs over the ocean then back to the house to start another fire in the stove and talk and plan again. To buy that piece of land, to live on it, to raise our own food. Needing so little, how could we fail? There were two ways to go about it. The sensible way, Ken said was *to stay here for another few months because there's plenty of room and Maggie insists that if we don't mind her being here, we're welcome to stay all summer. We can look at parcels of land, talk to people. I have a list of people who've moved up here. We can investigate, plan, move cautiously.* Or. I was the one who said it. Or we could just go and find out the price of the land we had seen, the beautiful place, our place, and buy it before (I didn't say this part) we thought too much about it, about how hard it might be, about how little we each knew, buy it because it was what we wanted and we must take it and then change ourselves to make us fit what we wanted. *And if it goes wrong?* I couldn't think about that, couldn't let Ken think about it. Too much had gone wrong for him and he had done too much thinking. We couldn't really talk this over and decide together because it was my money and he would hesitate and be afraid and if we didn't keep moving the way we were now, moving fast, away from where he was, there would be a sinking back. So we went to the real estate office and it was all done before Maggie came up at the end of the week, all but ten thousand paid for the hilly forty acres of Dago Gulch because it had water, a spring as well as a creek, and a level meadow and a road and *buildings* as the real estate woman said without a touch of irony in her voice though Ken said he'd have to tear down and rebuild everything but the stone house. We signed and it was done, done, though it took a few weeks to get all the paperwork completed and Ken had that little drinking bout with Marge and Burt on the day the deed came but never any other time, and by then we were already living here and working to fix it up. Ken working. Working. Could anyone ever have worked as hard as he did? Building and planting and watching over me till I got used to it so that I wouldn't break something or my own neck before I'd learned to be a real country woman in my thick boots, which were just right, which I now stopped dreaming about because the dream had come true. Love? Happiness? Is that what we have here with so much to do, so little time for anything but work and sleep, so that we live more and more in long, long silences, like the animals, like the trees, hardly talking except for the needed words, then the sound of our evenings only taped music ending at dark because we curl up asleep when the sun goes down. Love? *Work.* He said it like a prayer. He was the work and it was part—all of him, testing him, stretching him, swallowing him up so that there was no Ken anymore. There was only work and planning for work and resting from work, as if work had been stored up in him and now came pouring out with his sweat. All that Maggie said was there in him, all that I believed and knew somehow was there—was Ken. He grew strong and beautiful and his beauty came all around me and warmed me so that every word he said, every motion and touch came like music, right into me, becoming part of me—and I was the same for him, filling his music with mine. And is that love? Because if it is, we didn't have it when we started, we must only have had a hint that we could. We're still just starting, still at the beginning so it must grow into something so huge and fine and—but that's not true. It doesn't have to. It doesn't very often. Mostly it flashes and then—flickers out. Why? Other things, outside of us. Life. Everything. Yes, I know, because of what started to happen to us after the left-over money went for the jeep, the tools, the seed, the wire to fence the deer out of the vegetables, the planks and nails, the jars to put up food, the doctor—until we knew there soon wouldn't be any money left and there would still be the need for money, and the local people told us they'd never been able to live on the land, not entirely, no, they'd all had to take jobs in town, hard, dull jobs, as hard and routine as city work and paying less and lucky to get them. Ken said it would be all right, he wouldn't mind taking a part time job. Someone had already offered him work in a new bookstore opening up in Fort Bragg, only it paid less than his old job and Ken would have to drive two hours a day. I said nothing. I just listened and felt what he felt underneath what he said—that it was unfair because it wasn't as if Ken wasn't willing to work. No one could work any harder than he was working. But we wanted to stay here, working here together, going to help others on their land for a few hours a week, all helping each other. Not commuting to another store, to a city, to another rhythm, another way of life to make this way of living survive, but in saving it changing it, killing it. I saw something I never thought about before—that you could work with all your heart for something but the world wouldn't let you have it, something simple and good, something you have a right to. But out of your reach. Worse, I realized that was the way things happened, that most people in the world lived and died without having a bit of what was theirs by right. No matter how hard they tried. I saw why Ken had dropped out and lived the way he did for so many years after he found this out, lived with nothing but the cold knowing that he *wasn't hurting anyone.* And even that wasn't true. I knew that Ken had to have this now, his right to work at what mattered, now that he had made this complete change and opened up, letting this great store of energy break out, turning himself toward hope. *There's no middle ground for Ken. He's an extremist and life will go one way or the other, for Ken* Maggie said *with nothing between.* And knowing what might happen, what was beginning to happen, I was more afraid than

Coming up again. Rising. Up—up to—this is a strong one. Strong! Stop. Let go! Okay—okay—it's going. Think of pleasant things! Why do I start to think of good things and then let them get all muddled up and scared? Almost as scared as I was in August. So scared. But only for a little while. Only until Maggie found the answer. *A cash crop, that's what you need, like my dear old friends, Helen and Scott Nearing. They had maple syrup. A cash crop. So the first question is how much cash will you need?* We wouldn't need much because already in August we were eating mostly what we'd planted in March and next year there'd be more with chickens for eggs and a goat for milk and we didn't even buy coffee and could make our clothes last but there were doctor bills and things the baby would need.

And the taxes. So we worked and talked and figured. Until dark, when Maggie took her sleeping bag and went out to sleep on a bunk in one of the lean-to cabins or outside by the creek and came back cheerful, hopeful, trying to cheer us up in the morning. *I feel ten more years given me, just from sleeping under your stars, hearing your creek going by me, on and on. It must work! There's a way, I know there must be a way.* She found it while we were picking berries, climbing up the hill, far above our cabins on trails that really did become deer paths, and Maggie was going to show me how to preserve berry juice in jars. *You must start keeping bees too. Then you could sell the honey—though that wouldn't be enough of a cash crop, not quite. There must be something else that—oh. Oh, my dear, I think I've got an idea. There would be some difficulties but—the answer was right here all the time, I'm the answer, acting out the answer every moment I'm here!* She could hardly wait to get back for lunch when Ken would stop digging the root cellar and we could sit outside under the oak tree eating berries. *People like me, my dears, we're your cash crop. I know of several places already doing it. An old ranch outside Ukiah. An old hot springs further south. People like me, city people, not like you two, yet needing what you have here, in small doses.* Ken got up as if he was going back to his digging. *You mean a vacation resort? God, no. And even if we wanted to, it would take another hundred thousand to*. . . but Maggie snapped at him to sit down and listen and she really sounded like a strict school teacher you wouldn't dare to disobey. *You wouldn't change a thing except for a few repairs. Not a thing. Because that's the whole point. I'm not talking about having people here all summer getting in your way. Not at all. Just weekends. Groups of people for weekend retreats, seminars, conferences. And to work. Some will want to work, to learn what you're learning.* Ken started to make a noise but Maggie hushed him again. *No, don't be a snob. I know just what you're going to say about well-heeled academics coming up here to pollute the air with their fine ideas, like a poor man's Center for Democratic Studies. Besides, you won't get any of those. You'll get people who want a really remote place, a crude place where they camp out and eat plain food and get dirty and use an outhouse and rise with the sun and sleep when it's dark and dig in your garden. Maybe not even speaking all weekend. I know a man who has been looking for just that. Or maybe a group will come, people who work together and need to get away from the city, to get to know each other a different way. Just weekends in the summer. I think it will do—will give you barely enough. And you mustn't be a snob, Dear Ken, mustn't be too, too pure. The city still exists and we who live in the city need what you can give. Your bit of nature, wildness, quiet. Your roughness. And, truth to tell, all the cabbages you can grow here will not do as much to change the world as the bit of peace and quiet and clean air and real dirt you bring people to for a few weekends a year. That is, if you're still the Kenneth I know and didn't come here just to abandon the world!* Then she was quiet and Ken got up and went back to his digging. But when he quit at dinner time, he came into the house talking as if they'd been arguing all afternoon. *How would I get people to come here? I don't know any...* but Maggie just said *I do and they'll take my word and try it. Then it's up to you to see that they like it.* Then he started rattling off the practical questions. *How many can we handle? We'll have to haul in some of the food.*

They have to bring bedding. I won't let them smoke here and fifty other things all ending with Ken saying he couldn't imagine anyone being willing to drive that road. *Not I, my dear, but they'll love it because it makes it all seem so remote.* So they argued for the next two days until Maggie left. Then he started arguing with me and I was even tougher than Maggie because I saw this was a real chance and I saw that he wanted me to convince him. I said it wasn't good for us to be alone all year, that if he was sick of talking to people, I wasn't, I'd only just started and I hoped someone would bring a group from the Homer Center and places like it because handicapped people end up sitting inside four smooth walls, alone. Then we sat down and tried to figure out exactly how much money we would have to make so that we could stay here and it looked like a few hundred dollars on ten weekends in the summer would be enough to keep the jeep running, pay doctor bills and taxes, buy clothes and whatever food we couldn't grow. *We'll need another outhouse. Have to rebuild three of the lean-to cabins and run another water pipe out to a central washing area.* Next day he was digging harder and faster than ever, taking notes, writing down everything I suggested even though we thought we weren't starting anything till we came back in the spring. As if he somehow knew that Maggie would come back two weeks later and ask if we wouldn't like to try just one weekend before winter. There was this choir director, *dear old Ralph, going on tour with his choir but when they come back at the end of September he wants them to have a quiet weekend, a retreat before they start rehearsals for their winter season. Someplace primitive and remote but not too far to drive from San Francisco. A place where there are no telephones or candy machines or swimming pools or bars. Just dirt and birds and a running stream. It would be a chance to try it out, my dears. Shall I tell him yes?* So we worked out the prices and Ken ordered the food and dug a new outhouse and fixed the lean-to cabins but was still working on the pipes when they all came so they pitched in and helped and cooked the food themselves on open fires or ate it raw. And sang. Sang the whole weekend. They had just performed PSYCHE and they walked around and spread themselves out, some down by the creek, some way up the hill and then started, *Amour! source de toute vie* like the water and the hill and the sky singing. *Like the invisible voices in the garden of Eros,* Ralph said. *You must rename this place. It is the Garden of Eros.* But Ken said that name was a bit too fancy for us yet. *Wait till we're sure it won't all disappear as it did in the myth.* He laughed when he said it so I knew he'd stopped being afraid it would. He was happy singing with them while he worked so hard he barely had time to touch me as he ran past. And we cleared three hundred and eighteen dollars and Ralph made a reservation *for the first weekend you're open next spring* so we knew we had found our cash crop and that everything would

There it comes. What's wrong, Ken? Five minutes? Six? Something must be—hurts! Ken, where are you? Hurts—more—Ken, why aren't you—easing—easing. Why? Of all times! You saw enough of Maggie all weekend. Couldn't you just let her . . . an accident? That shower came just after he left. The road would be slippery. He could have gone off, he and Maggie, the jeep rolling over and over on top of them, dead, both of them—stop that! A breakdown. Flat tire. Motor trouble. Ken walking all the way to town to get help, to get a ride for Maggie. Or he could—he could be—no, I don't want to think that. Burt and Marge. He drove Maggie to her car then started back, met Burt on the road just like that other time, gave him a ride because of the rain, then went in and they gave him a drink and—don't think about that! Well, I have to think about it, if that's what happened and he's up there sleeping it off all night and I have no way of getting out of here unless I walk. Six miles to the main road where I could get a ride to the hospital. If I have to walk I should start now. Could I walk that far before—but I would have to start now unless—maybe when I thought I heard the jeep, maybe I did. Maybe he came back and—the choir people had gallons of wine, were always offering some to us but Ken never—suppose they left some. Oh, now that I've started thinking this way I can't stop. They could have, just like the people at the wedding. And Ken came back all tired and tense and afraid the way he is when everything goes well, when he succeeds. And he saw the half-empty gallon outside in the tub where they were keeping the drinks cold and—he could be out there now, ashamed for me to see him till he sobers up. Or passed out, lying there on the wet ground. I know I heard the jeep. I heard it, that noise and scrape. It must be out there now. Open the door. Ken? How cold it is. Shut the door fast, leave some of that heat inside and just stand out here and listen for a minute. Wind shaking the trees. Stopping. Shaking again, grabbing, whipping back and forth, a million leaves brushing each other, shaking off water. Then stopping. Still. Pat. Pat. A few drops of rain. Starting again? Big drops, a splash onto my face, one big drop like a handful splashed over my eye, another, then the wind again, no raindrops, then still. Still. Ken? Ken! Are you here, Ken! Crazy blind woman standing here calling. Alone. Alone? I don't know. I always know if Ken is near, always know just where he is. But now I'm too scared to know anything for sure. I can't feel and know. Ken? He could have gone to one of the lean-to cabins. Stretched out on a bunk. That's where they probably left the wine, a half gallon of it, standing in the corner of one of the cabins. And Ken drank it down like water, the way he did that time after the wedding, just pouring it down like a dose of evil-tasting medicine that he hated but needed. I can find him in one of the cabins. The path is even easier when it's wet, my boots sinking in soft muck, what must it be like when winter is really here, with real rains? And snow? Sometimes a little snow, they say, but usually melting off as soon as it hits the ground, more mud, more slush. Ken? Feel all the bunks. No, not here. I'd hear him breathing if he were. Or would I hear anything? Not thinking, not hearing. Calm. Be calm. Ken, are you here? Up the path, sixteen steps and a curve, ten more, I know it like a book. Ken? Not in this one either. Climb higher. Slower. Breathe. Out of breath. Never out of breath this way, no matter how pregnant. Scared? Third cabin. Not in here. One more. Level path just off to the side. Take it slow. A pain coming? No, just my imagination. All my imagination. Not here either. Ken? No, not here, and I'm standing here like a lost, crazy woman, hair all blown wild in the wind, standing halfway up the hill with my face turned to—splash! Huge drops of rain telling me to get inside, stop being so stupid. Climbing all over the slope when I could have just gone down to the old fence post where Ken always parks the jeep. It will be parked right there if he has come back. Now take it easy. The path is getting slippery, boots getting mud-caked soles. Don't want to slip and roll down there. Not so fast, half-running as if something is chasing you, trees whispering about you, telling it from their top leaves, spreading the word—crazy woman loose in Dago Gulch, bad luck place, something sad sure to happen there. Tell the deer, warn the squirrels and rabbits and skunks while the birds hide silent under leaves on the tree branches because they always know things first and they watch with their heads cocked, asking, wondering, is it true she's gone mad already? No, just stupid, just dreaming crazy, stupid things because she's not grown up and how can she take care of a baby if she's still a baby? Stupid. Because look, here's the fence post and you can march back and forth and all around it and the parking space is empty. No jeep. No Ken. He's not here at all and you just came out here and got yourself all cold and wet. Wet. You ARE a baby, so scared you wet your pants. Oh, how stupid, get yourself back to the house and change before Ken drives in and sees you standing here like a lost baby in wet overalls. Outhouse first. Stop at the outhouse. Here. That's it. Now you're inside, sheltered. Sit down and rest until you're empty. Quiet. Rain drops hit one at a time, slow soft taps, like birds landing on the little roof, quieter than the metal roof on the stone cabin. Soft, quiet, all protected by close, dark walls like a little playhouse, like the kind of place I loved to crawl into when I was little, when I made a little house of my own out of anything I could find. A huge cardboard box, with a tiny little window cut in where I could look out, just through that tiny slit and see people while I sat on the bottom writing a letter. Who was I writing that letter to?

It wasn't to a person. To something more than a person. I didn't know who or what. And I couldn't write much yet so it took me a long time just to write I AM HERE. CEYLON. Then someone, one of my sisters I think, looked at me over the top of the box, her big head smiling and laughing down at me and I saw I didn't have a roof, didn't have anything to cover and protect me so the next time I made my house under the dining room table where nothing could come down on me from above and I hung sheets and curtains all around so that it was like a tent with a solid roof and no one could surprise me. But it was so dark that I couldn't write letters to something-more-than-a-person so I only sat there very, very still, Jack and the Beanstalk, hiding while the giant walked around and around and never saw me. Staying very still or else the giant would remember me, find me, eat me, staying there so long that I didn't know I had to go to the bathroom until all of a sudden I moved and it was too late, I had wet myself and the floor like Dad's puppy that he finally killed (but that was years later) and started crying and the wife of the giant heard me. *What's the matter?* My mother pulling back the curtains and

Hold my stomach, hold this pain, grab it and—count again. See how long they're getting, four five six seven eight nine ten eleven twelve thirteenfourteenfifteensixteenseventeeneighteen too fast? As if to make it go away faster? Slow down. Twenty - two - twenty - three - twenty - four - twenty - five - twenty-six—that was the top. Going down now, fading away, taking just about as long going. So the contraction lasts almost a minute. Do they get longer? I can't remember, didn't Ken read something about that to me?

Intervals get shorter, pains get longer but only up to—wouldn't get longer than—that one wasn't bad. Holding my stomach like holding the baby, feeling it tighten, get hard. It got so hard that—what's that? Thin, slippery line across my hip like a silky thin ribbon, like a scar, like—that must be a stretch mark. I must have more, can't feel more, just that one mark. A mark. I am marked. They fade, Mom said, but they don't ever go away. A mark from stretching more than my skin could stretch, a wound. The first. No, being blinded was the first. But not like this. Going blind was an accident, not a natural thing, but this, this stretch mark is a normal, natural thing, a wounding, part of the wearing down of my body. I will wear down little by little until I die. I. Die. Never really believed that before. Die. How silly. I found a stretch mark and I think about dying. Feel death close. Can't help it, makes me shiver. No, it's the cold and wet that makes me shiver. Just get back into the house and hope that fire hasn't died. Pants wet and clammy, no, I won't put them on, just run to the house without them. Not run, walk, fast but calm, feel too heavy even to walk fast. But steady, no more panic, no more being stupid and afraid even if I am afraid. I can be afraid if I have to but I don't have to do anything stupid about it. Just get myself back into the house. Here. Good, so warm and cosy, good, put more wood on the fire. More, it'll take one more piece. Hang the wet pants on the chair right in front of the fire. Towel near the sink to dry my legs. Still wet? Why? Not raining hard enough. Water, water still running down my leg. Not pee. I didn't wet my pants or yes I did, but I didn't pee. Water. The water has broken. No, not broken, just leaking out. That's normal. Yes, I remember. Which book? Yes, the water sometimes starts to leak.

So if I put on another pair of pants, I'll just get them wet too. Oh, God. Fear coming up in me again. Like icy arrows up my veins. Why? Just because of a little water. Perfectly normal. Strange but normal. Pull a blanket off the bed, wear it, wrap it around shoulders. That's it. Now sit down on the chair by the nice warm fire. Put the towel under me, there. Now just sit still and quiet and calm and let the fire warm me up, melting the icy arrows. Look at the fire, see, look, I can see tiny, thin streaks of light, fire burning high. I always feel good when I can see those little streaks, lights, like little reminders that all the world is still there with me even if I'll never, never—stop that! First afraid. Now feeling sorry for myself! Warm up and think. Get my mind cleaned out so I can think. Everything will be all right. Everything will be all right. Everything will be all right. Ken will come in plenty of time. We will put everything into the jeep and go out on the road. We will drive very carefully over the wet road in our jeep with the wide, deeply-grooved tires that won't skid, won't slide, won't ever—hardly ever. We'll drive straight to the hospital. Ken with me, staying with me all through and the doctor too. And nurses. And all the help I need, pain killers if it starts to hurt too much. But it won't. It's not really bad. And I'm big and strong and very healthy and *everything is as normal as can be* said the doctor just last week. In a few hours it will all be over with and we'll have our baby, our Maggie, but I'll call her Margaret, don't really like the sound of Maggie. Then I'll be flat and quick again with my own body back plus a few stretch marks no one will ever see. Only three days in the hospital and I'll go back to Maggie's house where she'll stay with us for a couple of weeks *or less or more, until you feel quite strong and want me out of the place, at which time I'll go back to Berkeley and you two can stay in Mendocino till spring, till you're ready to tackle your wild place again.* We'll be warm and comfortable all through the winter and on dry days Ken will go back to our place and start more repairs because he won't be able to wait for spring now that he knows what we're going to do. And I'll stay in Mendocino and nurse the baby and play with it and on fine, sunny days go for walks and on cold days sit by Maggie's pot-bellied stove and sometimes she'll come up to see us. That's how we'll pass the winter. When spring comes we'll go back to Dago—no, we'll give our place a new name, a good luck name, maybe the one Ralph suggested—back to our Garden of Eros in time to plant the beans and squash and tomatoes and I'll learn how to milk a goat, learn so many new things. With plenty of time to get the place in shape before the summer weekends when we have people, starting in May with the choir again, and with Maggie's promise *don't worry, I'll have other groups signed up by spring.* So Ken won't have to go to a job in town. The people will come to us. The work will all be here and we can stay together, Ken and I and the baby, working hard, hard, but making a new life for us, better than either of us thought just a few months ago. If anyone had told me that before the end of this year I would be here! Best of all for the baby. Starting right from the beginning with fresh air and love and dirt and open green, *trailing clouds of glory* which is all I can remember from the ninth grade but Ken recited the whole thing for me from memory and I told him we musn't let anything take away the clouds of glory from our baby but he said he supposed all parents started out with that idea. But we'll do it. We will! *At least we'll try.* Yes, we'll try. Even if Evelyn's right and we don't love each other, if Ken needed money for a new start and I needed a sighted man, even if that could be true, we're starting to love each other, building something, two new lives, soon three, when our baby

Five minutes. Hurt coming while I—sit—wait. Hurts. Swells—swelling like—like trombones in Bruckner. Go away! Go—away. Shrink. Going away slowly as if it wants to stay—hold—hurt me. Gone. And I sit all hunched up under a blanket, wiping the wet off my shivering legs and—doing nothing. Nothing. There must be something—straighten up, stand up! Every time I move I leak. But I can't sit still. The wind moves, like the trees, like the creek. Moving. I want to keep moving too. That's good for me, the book said so. But does it make it happen faster? Don't want things to happen too fast before Ken can get back and get me to the hospital and—it's all right, a little pacing back and forth. Won't hurt me. Won't speed up the clock in me. That clock in my body has been set and the alarm will go off in so many minutes, over and over and sooner and sooner. I didn't set that clock, didn't decide the baby would come out now and nothing I do is going to change the way that clock is set in my body. My body. This body. Not mine anymore. Never was? I thought it was mine, but now I know that was never true. It always had its own way, its own laws, its own plans. Eight paces to the door, turn left, five paces to the big window. Three more to the bed, turn. Ten paces to the sink, turn, three paces, turn, four paces, nice and warm standing in front of the fire again. Eight paces to the door. Tiger pacing in a cage? More like an elephant. Back and forth like the day Evelyn and I marched back and forth in front of the movie house. But that was pacing for a purpose. This—Evelyn wouldn't pace back and forth this way for nothing. She wouldn't keep pacing and waiting for someone who's not going to come and when he does come will be too late. Everything will be all right? No! Something's happened. Something. Don't know what but I won't find out by pacing back and forth and getting worn out walking, wondering, waiting. I should get out of here while I still have time. Get clothes on. Dry pants out of the box. Stuff the towel between my legs, pants on, Ken's sweater over my shirt. If I can walk back and forth here, I can walk on the road. Only six miles. Ken's rain parka. There. Out the door. Shut. Just a few big drops, windy but no real rain. Down the path. Six miles to the main road where I can hitch a ride. This time of night? Not many cars will—only need one. Better than sitting there daydreaming and pacing and worrying. Probably meet Ken on the road halfway there and we'll get to the hospital faster. But if I have to walk all the way? Should have put something on my head. This wind! Pull the parka up over my head. There. If I have to walk it—six miles I could normally walk in three hours. Normally. All right, if I'm slow, maybe four hours. I have that much time, plenty of time. The doctor said several hours after the pains are five minutes apart. I can do it. I can—but I'm so slow! Getting out of breath. Slower. Tight and heavy down where the baby is. Feels different from—the baby's so low and heavy and—my back! Hurts when I walk. Not like just pacing back and forth in the house. I can't take long steps, can't take fast steps. Feel out of breath already. Just because I'm scared? Never walked the road alone before. No danger as long as I keep close to the bank, to the hillside. Keep my left hand touching the side, the rock, the brush, tree branches. They hit my face. Keep right hand up in front of face. No, off balance. Don't stay so close, just close enough so that my left arm touches a branch, twig, not even touching. There, now I'm getting it, feeling sense of mass without touching. It's there, I feel or hear it or whatever it is they say I can do. It's there, the high bank of dirt and rock and bushes, and I don't have to touch it to feel it, just have to believe I can, relax, don't be afraid. Almost as easy as when Ken and I walk down the road almost a mile every day just at sundown. I hold Ken's arm and take big strides, free, so free, not having to think about where I am going. Freer than he is because he is responsible for me, guiding me, watching, while I'm free to not see, holding his arm, matching his strides, moving in step, in a rhythm like dancing, like floating, with the ocean of air washing over me, waves of green smells full of bird's last chirps before dark and soft rushing of the stream below, moving just like us but in the opposite direction, rushing to meet us but always missing us, passing us by, rushing. And the flutter underneath all the other sounds, the flutter of little animals getting out of the way as we come along, our four thick-booted feet thudding into earth—that's how it must seem to them though we try to walk light so we can feel and hear everything and sometimes we stop while Ken tells me about something he sees. *That branch must have been broken in a storm. Now it leans over, across the larger tree, and some kind of vine has grown around it, twining out between the two trees. Right now there's a squirrel sitting there watching us, trying to decide whether to ignore us or run away, oh, there he goes. Flashed his tail at us and ran, but only a few inches. Now he's under the branch of the big tree, watching us again, frozen still, thinking we won't see him, watching us go by.* Then we start moving again, Ken saying *You know, I have begun to look at things again. I see more than I have for a long time. Maybe I see more than I ever have.* Making him tell me everything he saw, wishing to see and trying to imagine and asking questions is good for him too. I love the way he hesitates and then chooses just the right word. The exact, precise word to sharpen a picture so that it is almost clearer in my mind than it had been in my memory, which went back to a time when I never really looked much at things, when I was just like most other sighted people who never see much but only

Here it comes. I'll keep on walking through this one, pretend it's not—oh. No. Wait. My legs. I can't—hold this tree branch. Hold. Dizzy? No—wait a minute—hold! There. There—it's going. But strong. Stronger than the last—cramping my back—legs. Because it's so cold out here. Raindrops getting heavier. Oh no, starting to pour! And how far have I come? Don't think about it, just step out and keep going. Forward march. Forward creep? Legs don't want to take big steps. Wind. Legs so wet. Is it the rain or does the walking make me leak more water—all wet and rubbing and—this rock. I know this rock. Sit down. Rest a minute. Breathing so hard. This rock is only a few yards down the road. At this rate it will take me forever to walk six miles, to walk even one mile. Never reach the main road, have the baby out here in the mud on this road. In pouring rain. Then there'll be another story for people to tell about Dago Gulch, that hard luck place where that blind woman had her baby out on the muddy road and they both died of—stop it. Think. Rain has really started. They told us how this road gets in a heavy rain, slick in the hard places and mucky in the soft, sliding and sinking. Ken couldn't drive it. He'd have to stop somewhere, at Burt and Marge's cabin, somewhere, to wait. I won't meet him on the road. So this is stupid. A good idea if I had done it hours ago when I felt the first pain, but now—well, hours ago I thought Ken would be back in plenty of time and there was no reason to think of walking anywhere. But I can't walk now. Nothing to do but go back to the house. Where I'll be alone. No one to help. No—stop that. I'm not going to cry. I'm going to get up. Right. Turn around, right hand touching the branches, start walking back, forward march. Take a giant step, mother may I, no, you may take one baby step. Two. Three. Keep moving. Keep tapping my hand on the twigs, leaves, rocky side of the hill. Like when I was a little girl, walking along the street touching every telephone pole, pretending I was a magical robot taking electricity from each pole, until we moved to another tract where the telephone lines were underground and there was nothing but wide streets and flat lawns and no trees had been planted yet and by the time they were, we were moving again. That was when I had to give up electricity and invent a friend from Mars who went with me down the wide, flat streets, protecting me from the lawns which would swallow me up if I set foot on one. My friend Zinka was, like all Martians, purple and two feet tall, but could assume any identity she (sometimes he) wanted. Sometimes Zinka was the gray cat who lived next door and sometimes the footstool (the only piece of furniture we kept when we moved) and sometimes a bush that grew outside my bedroom window and sometimes a finger puppet I made out of a piece of purple paper, wrapping it around my finger and drawing a face with three eyes on it. Zinka knew and understood everything I was thinking. But I would tell her anyway because he was glad to listen to anything I had to say. And Zinka could do anything. Sometimes s/he would offer to vaporize someone I didn't like, someone who had been mean, like the neighbors who yelled at me if I played on their lawns, which was the real reason I couldn't set foot on them. But after talking it over Zinka and I always decided to give people another chance. Then—sometime, somehow, Zinka was gone. Disappeared. I can't remember when or why. Gone and forgotten. Till now. Gone with my childhood, I guess. I grew up? I don't feel grown up. I could use Zinka right now, just for tonight. I badly need a friend but I guess I'm too old for Zinka. Another friend. A woman? Man? Neither. Or both at once. If I'm going to invent a friend, I don't have to narrow it down to a man or a woman. My friend, what does it look like? Invisible, of course, an invisible friend for a blind woman. Where? Beside me? In the twigs I touch? Waiting for me back in the stone cabin? Why not everywhere? Not just in one place at a time, like Zinka. Here. In the cabin. In the rain. Everywhere. A name? Any name I feel like using. Or no name at all. Is that all right? Yes, everything is all right with my friend. I can tell it anything and it already knows. Knows much more than Zinka did, not only knows everything I'm thinking, but much more. Everything. Very wise and old but young and innocent too. Never bored with anything I say, never impatient. Loves me no matter what I say or do. Loves me much more than I love it or Ken or anything because—it can, and it understands that I'm just starting, can't love much yet. Has always loved me even before I invented it! Always will. And knows me. Knows everything so that I never have to explain. Look, Friend, if you know everything, you must know where Ken is. When is he coming? No answer. Just because you know everything, that doesn't mean you always tell. But you love me and understand and you're going to help, Friend, you're going to make everything all right. Yes. Yes. You're already helping to make me strong enough to walk back to the stone cabin. Left-right-left-right, very steady. Now, please, Friend, get Ken and bring him here in the next hour. Stop the rain so he can get over the road and get us to the hospital in time. Yes. Yes, thank you, the rain is already a little bit lighter and here's a wide, flat place where—yes, here's the post near the jeep parking place and in a minute I'll be out of the rain and in a warm house, warm, tight, stone cabin with rain only a clatter on the metal roof. Now, Friend, one more thing, get me up the path and into the house before—no, before the next—oh, no, please don't let

Hold on to the post—just hold—not too tight, want hands full of slivers? Besides—lean on it—books said relax—re—lax! Hang—on—there, here comes—the worst! Now it'll go. Less—less—just as sure as it came, it will have to go. Gone. Relax. Relax? How can I relax, standing in the rain and holding on to a rotten old post, talking to an imaginary friend, like a crazy woman, an imaginary friend who's no friend of mine! Wouldn't even hold off the next pain till I could take it in my nice warm bed. Let go, get moving, left-right. Can't expect Friend to help when I call it imaginary. I never called Zinka imaginary until—yes, when I finally did, s/he went away. I'm too old for imaginary friends. Oh, I don't want to be. I want to be a child and have—but I'm not a child, can't be, had a birthday, twenty-one years old, remember? Grow up. Be sane and adult. And alone. No. Not tonight. Not until Ken comes and the baby is born and we're all safe. Until then, no matter if it's childish or even insane—I need you, Friend. Not imaginary. Real as pain. All right, Friend? Real Friend. Help me up the rest of the path. Windier now. Is the rain getting heavier again or is it just the wind, pushing it against the slope, against me? A little rain never hurt anyone. Soon I'll be . . . a few more steps . . . good thing you told me to turn back. I would never have been able to make it through that uphill part of the road. Between the pains, I feel normal, but I'm not. The baby is far down there, almost between my legs, and everything in my body is working, working it down, down, and doesn't want to do anything else. The door! Oh, good, inside, get inside, quick, slam. Oh. Now if only the fire hasn't gone out. First of all, the fire. Heat still coming from it. Smoldering. Get it going again, build it up. Where is there a bit of flame? Can't see a thing, anything that could flare up again? A hot place? Strip of paper. Shove the paper in there, and there, and there, and please, Friend, let the fire still be—never mind, no begging for this and that. If I have to start it again, I'll just—there! Flare up! Now some wood, small pieces first. Ouch! Careful, all I need now is to burn my hand! Well, I can still laugh anyway, can't I, Friend? Now, one big piece on top. Not too big, don't drop it too hard or . . . okay, it's okay, it's blazing up fine. Now get out of these wet clothes. Just drop them. Shivering, shaking. Crawl into bed. Pull the covers up over me, curl up tight, the way the baby is curled up inside me, all warm and safe. Think about being warm. Warm thoughts, a warm time, like my birthday, Friend, remember my birthday? The twenty-ninth of July, so hot that Ken started working at five and quit for the day at noon, the only time he ever quit so early. And we sat under the willow tree down by the creek, both of us worrying about whether we would make it, whether we'd be able to make a real life here because that was before Maggie had invented our cash crop and after we realized we were running out of money. We thought about the same thing but we said nothing. We dipped our bare feet in the water to cool off, then took off our clothes and slid into the water the way we did the first time we came here. Then we came out again to lie on our backs in mottled leaf shade, looking up into the tree, Ken saying how the sun sparkled behind and through the leaves of the tree like a great secret force behind the leaves, behind everything, shining in and through everything. I could see it too, like clusters of tiny bright stars in a black sky, a hot black sky like a warm blanket, ripped, with white hot flames stabbing through the rips, piercing hot rays. Then we made love with me above because of the baby, because of the hard ground, *because I can look up and see you and the tree branches lifting behind you and the brightness pouring through them and tangling in your hair, making a flaming halo all around you.* Melting together into each other and into the reaching trees and the hard ground and the streaming flames of sunlight. Becoming part of all of it, more, deeper than the first time, when I had pulled us under the water, now so full of, so inside of everything that we weren't ourselves anymore and both of us were afraid even to speak and didn't for the rest of the day, until at sunset a fat old blue-jay squawked at us and Ken laughed and started to talk again but not about the way he felt under the tree. And I wouldn't say what I felt, what I knew. That I would die here. I was so happy. I thought it meant—I thought you were telling me, Friend, that we would win, would manage to stay here and make our lives here, that we would grow old here and then would die here together. I didn't realize that you might mean something else. That none of these things might happen, that I wouldn't grow old but might just die, die very soon, without

Pain . . . again.

Does dying hurt like this—swelling up like this—through to—my back—no—not really in my back—down to—no, up—there now, getting less—dying—what was I thinking? Dying. Why? Why think of dying? Ken and me. Warm Day. Lovely memory—then all of a sudden, nothing but the pain and me, pain in me, pain. Talk to me, Friend. Sounds. I need sounds. Vivaldi ended a long time ago. More music. But I just got the bed warmed up. I'll get cold. Make a choice, stay warm or get cold, get music, then get warm again. Music wins. Get up, that's it. Throw another piece of wood on the fire while you're at it. Now, the box of tapes, the very top box. What? Bach? Schumann? Something to bring back that warm, lovely memory of Ken and me out under the tree by the—here it is, the PSYCHE tape. Perfect. The first music Ken and I heard together. Pretend he's here, telling me the story. Set the tape going, hurry back to bed, curl up, cover up, eyes closed, getting warm . . . getting warm with soft, sleepy music, Psyche asleep, alone, abandoned by her family, by everyone. Tell me the story, Ken, how she waits on the edge of a cliff, thinking she'll be taken by a monster instead of the god of love who loves her and is only waiting for all others to leave her alone before he sends the wind to carry her off to his garden, his world of love. How beautifully Ken reads or recites poetry. He knows enough poetry by heart that he can recite for hours and never repeat anything. Maggie made him learn poetry, she started him off when she was his teacher, twenty lines a week and when there wasn't enough time, she threw out the grammar lesson so everyone in the class could recite. No teacher ever made me memorize poetry. Too old-fashioned. At my school no one would do it. I wouldn't. We would hate any teacher who tried to make us. I would have hated Maggie? I always think how wonderful it would have been if I had had a teacher like Maggie. But if I had . . . tell the truth . . . would I have liked her? Or made fun of her? I know the answer. I would have been just like all the other kids. Didn't I try to be? Didn't I put all my hopes into trying and trying and trying to be like the others, to think like them, to look like them, even if it was impossible because I was six feet two inches tall with freckles and big feet and hair like copper wire? So if Maggie had been at San Jacinto High School, I would have called her a crazy old lady because the others would have. I would have called her dirty communist and would have thought everything she said was evil, dangerous. Because I was stupid. With an empty mind. No. A mind full of junk. Not full of learning and experience and ideals like Ken. Or like Maggie. What fine memories would she slip into and hide in if she was alone and waiting and afraid? Driving an ambulance, even fighting one time, in Spain. Chaining herself to a lamppost and yelling *Let women vote!* Getting arrested at a rally against World War I and just about every war since. That time she mentioned Sacco and Vanzetti and I didn't even know who they were. *Well, it was way before your time, my dear.* But it was before Ken's time too and he knew. He knew because he had learned about things like that. I never learned anything. Never did anything different from what anyone else around me was doing. I'm not even a real person. I'm like one of those characters in the comedies on TV, part of some so-called American family that lives in the suburbs and mows the lawn and fights with her parents but always makes up with them because they're so wise. Not a real person. Our lives were just like acting out the television programs we saw all the time. Except that we weren't wise or kind or funny or loving in that nice way. We weren't nice at all, we didn't love, we didn't even like each other. Mom and Dad didn't like each other anymore. My sisters fought all the time and they didn't like Mom and Dad. And none of them liked me . . . didn't hate me either. Didn't feel much one way or the other except that I was too big to . . . to fit in. Never said so. Never even thought so. They could do that, could shut off thinking about anything, could put their minds to sleep and live their boring lives. Close out anything that wasn't boring, anything that might open their lives, expose them, show that they were not like the television world at all, but crazy and weird just like the people they were always warning me to keep away from, not only in places like Berkeley but even in San Jose, in high school, where there were a few crazy ones who didn't try to be like everyone else and Dad seemed always to worry that I was secretly one of those, but he needn't have worried because I wasn't, I was just another boring person and if I hadn't gone blind

Starting sooner. Time? Five minutes? No, less. I would—pain—Pain——PAIN!

Like a dark curtain coming down, no, like thick, choking smoke—filling—filling up my mind—less? Clearing. Going. It just stops everything, slowly fills up, chokes up my mind, blacks out whatever I was thinking. Different from a cramp. Wider. Hurts more lying down in bed. Or does it hurt more because . . . it just does, and it'll hurt more each time until—don't think about it. Think about the music. Sleepy music with dreams, with the god of love, Eros whispering and telling her there will be more than the empty life she knows so far, something waiting for her. That's it, make a pleasant scene, like a play on a stage, like the fantasy scenes I see that Ken says are so much more imaginative than what—but he's wrong about me, thinking I'm different from ordinary people. Probably because I'm blind. People have strange ideas about blind people, that we are wise and calm and know things that sighted people don't know. But I know being blind just makes me minus one more thing from an ordinary, boring girl. No, my blindness added one thing. Money. The most interesting thing in the world to most people. Money. So here I was, this big, boring girl with the most interesting thing in the world. It made me fascinating to the men at The Center, like that one, what was his name? who was always playing loud records in his room and asking me to come upstairs and listen to them. He asked me to marry him the second time he talked to me, then told me all the plans he had for how we could live on my money. That was when I learned that everyone at the Homer Center knew I was getting some money and men started to hang around. It was a new thing to have boys, men, paying attention to me. So it took me a while, knowing they were after the money, before I decided to push them away and be lonely again. Greedy men. No more greedy than my father? Than my sisters? The second night after I came home they were there, without their husbands and children. At first I thought Mom asked them to come. She was always trying to make family reunions for Thanksgiving or Christmas. But it couldn't be a reunion if they came alone. To see me? But they hadn't called or written the whole time I was at The Center. I hadn't talked with them for so long, I couldn't remember . . . trying to remember what they looked like. But I couldn't imagine them, couldn't even tell them apart anymore. It was scary. Two voices, both the same, both just like Dad at a higher pitch, all his rough, restless, angry, cheated, craving fear. Just like him. As soon as they took a sip of the coffee Mom gave them, they asked me for money. Then I knew why they had come. One wanted to leave her husband. The other wanted to open a shop. I think. They never got a chance to explain before Dad jumped up and started yelling. *I should throw you two out. Tramps. Greedy bitches, try to take money from your poor blind sister like stealing it out of the cup of a blind man in the street!* That hurt me worse than my sisters wanting the money. How he hated me blind! How ashamed he was of me. And of himself. Yelling at them to hide his shame that he had spent almost thirty thousand of the money and already had plans for the rest of it. So they left and I didn't see them again until June when they came up here with their children, who played in the creek while I showed them around the place, Ken going on working because there was so much to do. *Oh, don't stop for us, let us help!* But instead of helping they asked questions and left long, long silences after my answers. They wanted to know if, blind and all, I had ended up happier than they were, because they were restless like Dad and trapped like Mom and they thought of leaving their husbands and coming up here to live with us. But they couldn't see happiness here, couldn't see anything we had but hard work, so they left after telling me that Ken was just taking advantage of me, that Dad was right, Ken had only married me for the money. When I didn't answer, they drove off. What was there to answer? Maybe they were right and Ken wouldn't have married me without the money. Why else should he want me? Ignorant, awkward, blind. Evelyn said it, the money meant a new life for Ken. Even Maggie loves me for what I can do for Ken. So . . . no one sees anything in me but money. No one. You? You, Friend? What do you see in me besides

Ow—curtain coming down on a bad scene—bad, ugly scene—hurts more than—pain—Pain! At least pain —goes away—but that ugly scene—there. Going. Make that ugly scene go—go away too. I don't care if Ken only wanted me for the money. He's been good to me anyway. He's been fine until—don't think about it. Listen to the music. Hear it? The wind music. The zephyrs carrying Psyche away, floating her away to her happiness. Soft wind, gentle and warm. Not like the wind outside, whipping the trees, shifting, shifting, never stopping. Cold, restless wind, always moving, moving. Like Dad. Always moving . . . to what? Noplace. Doing things that didn't mean anything, just to keep moving, moving. Once it was painting pictures. Painting by the numbers, filling in the little marked spaces. Number six was red, five was blue. I was little, but I knew my numbers and I watched him and thought it might be fun, but he never let me try. He painted and painted and framed and framed and hung them on all the walls, then bought more canvasses with blue lines and numbers. In the garage, at his easel, painting the little spaces as fast as he could, filling the little spaces and the dark corners of the garage. No more room to hang them. Then all of a sudden he stopped, bored, through with them. Threw all his paints into the corner with the paintings, with all the other stuff. All corners of the garage filled until there wasn't room for the car anymore, and it had to be parked outside, and that meant he'd soon get rid of it too. Garage full of boxed sets of ready-made things to do. Things he saw on TV and sent for—exercise equipment, sets of books, correspondence courses, motors, tools for assembling ready-made parts of things that never got put together. It would all pile up and pile up until he bought another new car, and the garage had to be cleaned out because for a while he'd want to keep the new car in the garage. Or until we moved again and everything had to be sold or given away. All ready-made things. Finished. Decided. Dead. Except for the time he decided to take up bonzai, after Mr. and Mrs. Izumi moved in down the street and he said we should move because the only good Jap was a dead Jap, he'd learned that lesson in the war and wouldn't forget it, but he did forget it long enough to let Mr. Izumi show him how to put little trees in pots and shape them, though he always called Mr. Izumi *the little Jap* behind his back, and I'm sure Mr. Izumi knew he did. Dad bought a bunch of little trees from a nursery owned by a friend of Mr. Izumi and a kit of tools that cost two hundred dollars and special soil and pots and a table to work on out on the patio. Mr. Izumi told me *Bonsai teaches patience, love of nature. We listen to the trees and work with them. Learn from them. We become better people.* But the trees and Dad never seemed to get together. I watched him twisting the branches, wrapping wire around them. He was too rough, impatient. He broke branches. Even the ones he didn't break looked funny. Mr. Izumi's trees were dignified old trees standing against the wind, light and balanced in their tiny, shallow clay pots, bending to keep standing, keep strong, saying, *Remember, remember, no matter what happens, we must live in beauty, grace and dignity.* But Dad's trees looked twisted and awkward as if they had been yanked up and jammed into the little pots, as if their roots must hurt like feet in tight shoes, as if they were fighting against the wire Dad twisted around them, silently and stubbornly protesting that they hadn't been listened to and shaped patiently, but forced and expected to turn graceful overnight. I guess Dad couldn't hear them. But he gradually realized . . . one night I heard him yelling at the trees the way he would yell at us when he had run out of things to do, and after that he never looked at them again. I watered them for a while, but then I forgot, and they silently died without—oh, stop it—I don't want to think about that. Every thought I make turns sad, every scene I put on the stage—back to the music, the music will always—listen, zephyrs gone. What's the next part, this grand, broad, beautiful—that's the Garden of Eros, where she wakes up—tell me that part again, Ken. *She wakes up in splendor, green and golden splendor.* Surrounded by love and mystery. But the music isn't like the story at all. Hear it? Not a pleasure garden, more. Hard and fertile . . . wide, more solid and earthy with dark strength from deep in the earth, rich with life, more strong and deep than the story ever

Coming again—spreading out—time? Four minutes? Less. Spreading—familiar now—now I know what—it—will—do! How much more? There. There. Going down—down. Down. Rain rattling the roof again. Almost drowning out the music. Strong music, stronger than rain rattle. Garden of Eros, much stronger than the story, hard and usable. Eros. Love. Passion? Endurance too. Mom would understand that music. She could endure and love Dad no matter what he did. She was the only one who could put up with him. Because he was as crazy as anyone at the Med, with voices worse than Davide's driving him, mean voices. If it hadn't been for Mom taking all of it, smoothing it over, comforting me and my sisters, apologizing to the neighbors—if it wasn't for Mom, he would be alone and drift out on some street, lost and mad, and after a while he'd be put away somewhere. Or become one of the old men on Telegraph, the sad ones, leftovers from no one knows what, the ones people tried to pretend weren't even there. But because Mom loved him so much . . . did she? Not when she was telling me to get an abortion. Not when she talked about marriage. She said things that meant she didn't love him anymore. Wouldn't leave him, but didn't even like him. Hadn't for a long time. Never did. Not while I was alive. Even when I was little and I used to look at that old picture of them together, him in his blue Marine dress uniform, his face soft and blurry, not sagging yet into those puffy pouches that swell up when he yells, and her face laughing. I would study that picture and try to see Mom and Dad in it, but I never could. They looked like an old movie on the TV late show, with the love scenes where the actors both turn their faces to the camera, touching cheeks, so you know they're just actors who are thinking about how they look. But everyone looks that way in pictures. You can't tell how they really feel. And everyone wants to be in love. Mom and Dad wanted to love. I guess. I suppose. By the time I came along, all that was over and Mom was just trying to keep everyone together and happy. Keeping Dad happy by giving in to him when he was mean. Then coming to comfort us. When I was little, I used to hear her in my sisters' room. They would cry and she would talk softly, softly. *Don't cry. Calm down, don't feel bad.* They would get quiet but not calm. For a long time not speaking to Dad, faces like stone, until both of them got married and left before they were eighteen and hated him still and go on hating him, sounding like him and acting like him and hating him. Then it came time for me to hate him, to feel bad when he yelled. Then Mom would hold me and talk softly. *Yes, I know he's like that, yes, I know how much it hurts.* Then I'd feel even more angry because he had been mean to her a lot longer than he had been mean to me and I thought she was a much better person than any of us because she never yelled back at him, never got angry. Didn't she? Yes, she did. It was hidden in there, somewhere in her hurt, patient look. Angry for herself, angry for us. *Yes, I know. Don't you think I understand exactly how you feel?* She was telling us we were right to hate him! Did she want us to hate him? Was that a good way to get back at him for all the mean things he did? A better way than just—I never thought—could it have been that way? Was she really fighting back all the time? Using us? Telling us he was wrong, but we were helpless, instead of telling him he was wrong. If she had ever yelled back at him, fought him right out, for herself, it would have been different. She just left him in the wrong, gave in and comforted us and told us, without saying it, to hate him. The best revenge, to make his children hate him. I wonder if that's why he seemed so crazy, so much worse than I remembered when I came home from The Center, why he felt cheated not to get all of my money, why he seemed furious and suspicious all the time as if some invisible enemy had beaten him, bruised him, tricked him, defeated him. I wonder if anyone ever liked Dad. Or if he ever had a friend. Or a Friend, like you. No, he couldn't have. Neither could Mom. If they had

Here it comes. Good. Better a pain than this—why can't I hang on to a good thought—coming up—a hard one—harder—back—GOING—oh, my back. There. Going. As soon as this one's gone I'm going to—what? Hungry. Eat something. There. I can get up. Easy. Dizzy? No. No. First another piece of wood on the fire. More, another, more, build it up as high as—careful, don't smother it. Better put clothes on. Ken's flannel shirt still hanging on the peg? Forgot to pack that. Good, comes down over my hips, opens around the baby. Won't get wet. Bed's damp. Should have—better put a towel in the bed, another. There, that's dry now. Something to eat. Hurry up, before—don't start shaking, calm down, there's time, move easy like the music, that lovely chorus part now just like the chorus singing this afternoon, on the hill, down by the river, singing at each other about love, the source of life, making the fields bloom. Lots of talk up here about making the fields bloom, but not with love, with fertilizer and water and all those practical—here, apple still in the cooler. Next year maybe a refrigerator. Freezer? We talk about that a lot, how much the old way and how much technology. Everyone does. Constant as the idea-talk at the Med, constant as the rain battering the roof, steady rattling but not so loud now, like part of the music. Get back in bed quick now, and think about those things. Chew the apple and think about septic tanks, chew this apple, chew it all up, get it down before the next pain. Will the pain make me throw up? Will it creep up my stomach, up to—think about nice clean things like fertilizer, compost, not pain, don't let in any more thoughts about how people hurt each other, how they live all twisted together in hate. Why? One of those little sculptures in Maggie's house, the dancing one, was called CHOOSE LIFE. Why don't people choose life, choose love? Is it so hard to love? Will I ever learn? Too hard? Mom and Dad living in their untouched department store window, everything always new, with no smell, killing each other day by day, choosing war, death instead of life. No better than those stoned people shuffling around Telegraph, not rebels, no more rebels, just lost people staggering and sitting on the filthy sidewalk, mumbling . . . *change.* Even Ken's old friends at the Med, so cruel to each other, calling each other names . . . *leftover garbage from the sixties.* When Madeline began reciting, *We are the new lost generation!* they all laughed at her and Davide asked *How many lost generations have you joined?* but they stopped laughing as she read on and on, a poem that described each of them with such sharp, cruel words, slicing their laughter to silence. Then applause. Then starting to taunt each other because they knew all the hurt, weak, wounded spots, the failures—the lost work, the bad poems, the deserted loves, the abandoned children, the half-finished novels that would have justified it all, the sell-outs, who had left the avenue and gone after jobs, status, money. Maybe they talk about us that way now, full of spite for anyone who left the circle of brilliant tortured spirits in that pure hell that was so much more interesting than ordinary earth. How Mabel Insell sniffed when she mentioned *those Telegraph Avenue types who are vastly inferior to our so-called handicapped here at The Center, who keep cheerful and neat and work so hard to overcome their blindness, to get a job, to lead a clean, normal life.* When nobody else could be normal, the people at the Homer Center were set on being . . . but were we any better? That time Mr. Canfield came to our abacus class and made us play his old game, what's good about being blind? To develop positive attitudes. What were the answers? *Because I'm blind my father gives me things my brother doesn't get* and *my wife will feel too guilty to leave me again* and *people never contradict me anymore* and Theodore's bragging *I've lived in six places like this in the last five years, all at government expense like a long vacation.* Terrible reasons to like being blind and Mr. Canfield—keeping a positive attitude—didn't even say so. And people up here aren't any better for all the fresh air and open space, with old, bitter feuds that go back years, only agreeing on one thing, that they don't like new people, and some of the meanest were new people themselves only a few years ago and had the same

Pain coming. Damn. Yes, just like life. All timed so you get a little space of time without—so you almost forget, until it sends the pain to creep up on you—and up—and up! The top? More? To fill you—and change everything to—reality! Pain, hurt and—going. Going now. Almost gone. Gone. Nothing at all now. But what good is that, when I know it's only for a few minutes before pain comes again, like a little happiness before everything turns into pain. There. It's there in the music, there, the chorus coming to that part, those awful four notes, that warning, letting her know that if she looks too close, she'll lose her happiness. I don't want to hear that part. I'll get up and eat more. No. Don't want to move, stay curled up, still and quiet till it creeps over me again. Quiet, like the few months of happiness Ken and I have had, dreaming of making such a good life for ourselves and then, then, then reality comes. Comes? It's always been there, waiting deep inside like the pain, waiting for me to forget. Then it swells up and oozes through me, through everyone. Didn't Mom and Dad think they would be happy instead of living longer and longer times of misery together with only short breaks like vacations? And Ken, with all his talent and education, half his life gone and it's been mostly unhappy. He can only be happy when he's working so hard that he forgets himself, doesn't even exist anymore so that he can't feel the pain. But even then the pain of reality builds up and up in him and would kill him if he didn't kill himself first, for a little while, with a bottle. Even Maggie. Even Maggie with her pacifism, her revolutions, her artist lover. Didn't everything fail? Didn't her love end up tortured to death and didn't her side, the good side, lose? Good side? Even Maggie stammers and mumbles when Ken asks her about prisons in socialist countries or how much money she made writing those capitalist movies or . . . Evelyn. Last of all, Evelyn. Last, because I don't want to think about her, the best, the strongest, the bravest. Never letting a good fight get away from her, or a good laugh. Never afraid. The only person I ever knew who was all alive, who chose life! And lost it, had it torn away from her. How do you explain that, Friend? Do you really think that's fair? Don't you think life ought to—or is that the message? Is killing Evelyn the way to let the rest of us know what it's really all about? Is that the answer to all the questions I ask you that you never answer? Is that why I'm still alive? Because I'm not like Evelyn, don't have her courage, or if I began with as much courage, it all leaked away a long time ago. The way Ken's courage did before *I got some back from you, Lon* as if he expects a little courage to grow like a seed into a plant. I thought so too, I guess. But now I'm beginning to see that it doesn't work that way, and maybe Ken and I are just being allowed to live so that the whole game of quiet and pain, quiet and pain, can be stretched out longer than it was for Evelyn. *Fix this place up, just a little every year, Lon.* But just a little every year means steady hard work day after day, through all the daylight hours. Steady, silent, sweated work, hard, with Ken pushing himself to the limit, past the limit, while I stand around helpless, useless. I told him I don't want him to do it all, that he doesn't have to prove to me he can do it alone and leave me sitting quiet and useless with earphones on, lost in canned music, helpless. *Not true, not useless!* Then Maggie chimed in with stories of another lover, a blind poet *who could do anything! My dear, you should have seen how he . . .* They sounded like Mr. Canfield at the Homer Center. Then Ken started, a couple of weeks ago, to have me work along with him. All I did was slow him down. I can't bend. And I drop things and then can't find them. He has to watch me while I'm feeling around to make sure I don't put my hands in a dangerous place. Or trip and fall. *You'll be better at it after the baby comes.* Good excuse. *Don't worry, it'll take time, but you'll get it.* Time. Years and years. And I don't have years to learn to take care of the baby. Baby. I'm a baby, a brat, complaining like this. That's what you think Friend. Complaining about everyone else because I'm worse than

Oh, no. Don't start. Please! I'll roll up in a ball, pull the covers up over my head so you won't find me, I'll get—oh, hide so it can't get me! Can't! it's INSIDE ME so I can't get away. Part of me. How can it—last—so—long! Hurt—so—much. . . and. . . then just. . . creep. . . away as if it never was. It's not right, is it, Friend? Are you listening? I don't think it's fair. Not fair! How do you feel about it? You're sorry for me. You agree with me, don't you, the perfect friend. Maybe you don't. The best Friend doesn't always agree, the greatest love can be. . . hard. Like Eros, leaving her for just one little mistake. Stern. But even if you don't agree, you feel the pain with me. You hurt with me. But what can you do about it? Nothing. Not fair. Nothing is. Nothing in my whole life has been fair, where I was born, the people I knew, nothing, nothing. I always knew it. So you decided to do me a favor. Or maybe I asked for it. Maybe I asked you, Friend, back when you were still only Zinka, maybe I said, take me away from here, away from living in this candy machine where I can only see the world through coin slots. I did, I wished a million times that I could stop trying to fit in, that I wouldn't any longer be the six-foot redhead Amazon of San Jose, waiting to marry someone like my father or to squeeze my big knees under a typewriter for the rest of my life.

And so, Friend, you granted my wish, didn't you? Just like the fairy tales. You gave me what I wished for, only, just like the fairy tales, there was a catch to it. And the catch was that I would go blind. That's all. A car swerving, a bump on the head, a beautiful purple-golden streak shooting through my brain and then going dim, dimmer, dark. Six weeks later I sit in the dark and wait for the big miracle. *Medical science!* Dad yells, fury and fear shaking his voice. But I wasn't waiting. I had forgotten all about my wish, about all wishes. I was just waiting to die, not expecting anything, not hoping, just waiting for the time to pass. I was all through with wishing. But my blindness was all part of the wish. That's how wishes get granted, isn't it, Friend? That's how new lives are made. You want, you wish for a new life? Yes. Wish granted. But first, one little thing. You go blind. Then a few more things. You try to die, you sit and sit until Mom and Dad are so crazy with looking at you that they have to do something, anything to get rid of you. If you were a dog, they could send you to the pound like the other one. But all they find is the Homer Center. And everything follows, just like the fairy tales, once upon a time this happened and then this and then . . . the Homer Center, Berkeley, Telegraph, Ken, the land. And here we are three hundred miles from candy machine suburbia, curled up in a cabin in the middle of nowhere, playing music drowned out by the pounding of the rain on a tin roof. That's how I got my wish! Couldn't be—nothing could be as different from San Jose as where I am now, how I am now. Oh, and one small price for this great change. My eyes. That's all. Blind. Blind girl. Blind woman. Blind old woman. Blind for the rest of my life. And this baby, if it ever gets born, will say *my mother's blind* and will be ashamed of me. Yes, yes, Friend, it will. Because everyone is just a little bit like Dad, a little ashamed, a little revolted. So, good old Mr. Canfield, wherever you are—are you meeting with some new students at the Homer Center now? Are you naming off your list of famous handicapped people? Helen Keller, Milton, Beethoven, Dostoevsky, Byron, and are you now asking the big question, playing the big game? *Tell me something good about being blind.* Well, I'll tell you right now, Mr. Canfield, and you too, Friend, though you must know it already. There's nothing good about being blind. Nothing. It's horrible and stupid. Being blind means I'll never see my baby, never see a million other things I'm starting to forget or never got to see, so that I'm even starting to dream blind, when at least I used to see in my dreams. And it means I'm a drag on people. Someone always has to do things for me, no matter how clever Maggie thinks I might become, and I can't get clever when I'm stumbling around, getting in the way. I don't even hear as well when people talk because I can't see mouths moving, and people don't want to talk to me anyway because I'm deformed, a freak, spoiled, maimed. I hate being blind, I hate it, and sometimes I get so mad I hate the world and myself, and I hate you too, Friend, because what kind of friend are you to let this happen? I wish I'd invented you as a thing with a body so I could get these hands on you and kill you, and then I'd kill Ken too and then

A hard one, coming fast. Cruel—mean. Cry? No. No! Go ahead and hurt me. Hurt—you can do better than that! Yes, that's—there—the worst. Can't get worse. Not yet. Not this time. It has to weaken. Weaken—and—slowly—go—go—and I didn't cry. Not going to cry. Too mad to cry. Never been so mad. Or maybe I always was inside, deep mad like that deep pain growing. But not shrinking again. Staying mad. Staying mad all the rest of my life. Maybe not a long time. Maybe I'll die. From this pain nobody knows but me. Not Ken. Not Maggie. Mom. She felt this pain. Three times. Left alone almost like me. Alone in a room in the hospital, with Dad downstairs in the waiting room. When I was born, he didn't even stay there, stayed at home till they called him. Nurses to look at her and see when to call that doctor at the last minute. Nobody but some other woman screaming next to her. She told me about those awful screams. But I'd settle for a screaming woman now, just not to be alone. I wish Mom was here. She's good at giving comfort to anyone trapped in pain. At least she knows. To have someone here who has gone through this, who understands—you understand, Friend, yes. But I want someone human, someone who's felt dumb human pain. Like Mom. Worse for her because she never wanted—at least I want my baby. Or I thought I wanted a baby. What do I know about it? Maybe Mom was right and raising children is a lot of hard work for nothing, nothing. Because look at how people turn out. All those cute little babies. What do they turn into? All those people at the Med, at the Homer Center, at San Jacinto High School—they were all beautiful little babies once *trailing clouds of glory.* Even Mom and Dad. They were babies once. Why do I find that so hard to believe? Think it. Believe it. Mom didn't want children, but even she must have hoped that I'd turn out better. She named me Ceylon. Because she wished she was far away? Because she hoped I would grow up beautiful and exotic and do the wonderful things she never did? So I turned out worst of all, a big, awkward, shy, sleepy girl who topped it all off by going blind, which really meant I'd be a baby forever and ever, never grow up to be anything at all, just a big baby for her to take care of for the rest of her life. A joke on the woman who wished for no children. Cruel like the jokes played by the gods in the myths. Like the jokes on Psyche, all the hard things to do that couldn't be done, yet when she found a way to do them, Aphrodite just made harder ones for her. Then laughed at her. Almost made her kill herself. Big joke. You, Friend? Your joke? No. Maybe my going blind was worse for Mom than for me. Too awful to face, so that she wasn't really lying about loving or not loving Dad and me. She just didn't know anymore what was real. Now she's free of me. But she's lost reality for good. Life is only . . . pretend. Those letters she started sending a couple of months ago, one a week, just like the ones she wrote me at the Homer Center. Never saying how I left with Ken and she wouldn't come to our wedding or how Dad tried to get a lawyer to take the money away from me, *incompetent.* Her letters just say they bought a new car, she lost eight pounds, she likes her new course at the college, Dad bought a computer he can attach to the television set and play games with. And she hopes I'm feeling well, getting good medical care and planning to have my baby in a hospital, *not at home the way some of these foolish girls do.* Then she finishes with *love to Ken* as if she knows him, as if everything between us is all right. Once in a while I write back a few words on a postcard . . . my excuse is that writing is hard when I can't see it. Does she take the card to friends and tell them she's going to be a grandmother? As if everything is all right? Just the way she has always been, with marriage, home, children, all pretend to cover up what life really is, the pain and trouble of having babies who grow up mean like their father or ugly, dumb, blind. When I was a little girl, I asked her does it hurt very much to have a baby? She wouldn't say yes. Had to keep pretending. But this one time she stopped pretending a little bit. This was too close to her for lying so she said *it's not a sick pain* as if

There—coming—don't tense up—listen to the music. No pain in—yes—pain in the music too—rising—rising—no—no! How can it—hurt—so much! Mom! Okay. Okay. Going. Mom was right. Not a—sick—pain. But it scares me, the way for a second there at the top I get lost in it . . . swallowed up. I feel . . . surprised that it comes on so slow but then grows so strong. It doesn't fit because when it's not there I'm fine, normal, just me. I can't believe this great pain is going to grow inside me, that it's waiting while I have forgotten it, while I can't believe in it because I feel fine, normal, not sick. Not a sickness, having a baby. Normal. A normal thing in the lives of women. So much more pain than when I was blinded. Hardly any pain then, knocked me out, a few headaches when I woke up, dimming lights, everything going dark soft and slow like sunset on a cool day. Couldn't believe my injuries serious. Maybe most people don't feel pain when they are hurt the most. Like Ken during all those years he spent saying no. Was it easy? Painless? Numbing, killing his brain, not hurting him, just quietly destroying himself with drugs and drinking *and the drop-out limbo of the streets.* Destroying brain cells with drugs. All those aching billions of brain cells. Friend, I thank you for letting him have so many left over so that he's still the most intelligent—but why should it be that way? Why should it hurt less to die and hurt so much to live and hurt the most to give life? *At first it did hurt to say no . . . and then it became habit . . . and then nothing hurt anymore. You made me start hurting again, Lon, you made me see it was time to try to say yes to something.* But then he would go back to warning me that he was unreliable, had made his commitment to non-commitment, had forgotten how to be consistent and I mustn't let him grab at me to pull him out because he'd only pull me in too, he'd only let me down, he'd only—so I'd tell him shut up, I won't listen and I could tell how glad he was to be stopped because the day before our wedding he called it *my worst self-indulgence, talking that way, and I give it up, Lon, for good.* But he was right, wasn't he? He has let me down. He's up there right now with Marge and Burt, a few more brain cells dead and the rest asleep, out, feeling no pain, not even knowing or caring about my pain. His little suicide when he can't keep pushing and dragging and punishing himself like one of those saints Maggie likes to compare him to. They beat themselves until they passed out and saw angels. Ken beats himself too. All the time that things are going well, all the time he's working hard and getting somewhere, all the time we're just being happy together, inside he's beating himself, beating and beating, until he can't stand any more and passes out, with a little help from a bottle. He's split, broken right down the middle. He cracked open when he was my age, just the way Maggie said *from the strain of the contradictions he was facing* and the split is like one of those earthquake faults that never heals but just sits there for a long time without any movement until strains build up until the crack opens and shifts and that's an earthquake. Like after the wedding. Like after we signed the papers for this place. Like right now. After our first successful weekend, after he knows something has gone right and he'll have to go on and on and live it and be happy and follow through and live! Then he cracks and shakes. Only for a few hours. A minor attack like an attack of malaria. In a few hours he'll be okay again, not shaking, nothing lost but a few hours. Nothing lost for him. But what about me? He said it, he warned me, he knew. He said he'd let me down when I need him most, when I

Stay loose! Don't let fear tighten—one of those books said go—with—it but—ohoo, did it say—book say to moan? No. Breathe. How? Pant? Now? No—no—noooho—does it help to moan? Just to do something. Some women scream. When will I start to—I never screamed ever in my life. Books said screaming is a waste of energy. Already too tired to scream. Wouldn't do any good. Too late for screaming. I should have run out on the road at the first pain, screaming, and Ken would have come back or someone might have heard me, someone else, even miles away. Sometimes I can hear when the wind is right, an animal, a dog barking miles away. No one would hear in this rain, this wind. Screaming would be for nothing, for no one but me. Alone in a different way from—more alone than when I first went blind. Lost. Just when I started to believe I'd never be alone again. Another joke on me, Friend? Standing there in the window holding up the candle, feeling proud to be so big, proud for the first time, proud of my height and the big baby sticking out. Holding up the candle and waving and thinking I did look like a statue or *like a goddess* Maggie said. That was when the first strong pain came, the first I knew wasn't just a stomach ache, came to stop all that pride and happiness and hope. Maggie's hope. She's the one who kept talking as if our life, our marriage, our baby, our land out here was something as great as Adam and Eve starting the world all over again. *A miracle, my dears, and one miracle leads to another, I'm quite convinced of that and you two make me think, no, truth to tell, you make me see and know that anything is possible!* Silly old woman! Probably getting senile. Why did she keep saying things like that? What made her believe that Ken and I could do it? Two losers, handicapped. An ignorant blind girl and an aging drop-out. With the usual daydream about going Back To The Land. *You folks pretty late. They been coming back to the land more than twenty years now.* That old man at the hardware store gave us sad grunts and chuckles with his advice about farming because he knew what had happened to most of the other people who tried. We knew too. They're back in places like Berkeley again, on the streets or waiting on tables or getting more degrees or taking the jobs and money they said they never would and feeling sad and comfortable, comfortably sad. The few who stayed are working at the mill or if they're lucky teaching at the grammar school and saying how the new people are spoiling their countryside. So Maggie should have known better than to think we could make a new and better life here. Hasn't she been in enough lost causes? From the time she was younger than I am! She can name more lost causes than Mr. Canfield can name handicapped geniuses. So why couldn't she take one look at us and see—that's it. She knew just what she was seeing. We're another of her lost causes. Sure. We fit right into her life, another lost cause, a small one, just the latest in a long line so that Maggie can keep her life going along the way it always has. That must be why she loves Ken. Because he's a lost cause, brilliant and broken. The two of us, what a pair! She can believe in us the way she believes in socialism and pacifism and human rights and—that scrapbook she keeps. Ken read me the clippings. Maybe she'll add our wedding pictures to that scrapbook and —oh no, Friend. I can see that frown on your invisible face. No, no. How will I feel if it should turn out that the jeep ran off the road and rolled over and over and Maggie and Ken are lying on the rocks at the bottom moaning like me, no one to hear them. Or quiet, dead, rain pouring down on them. How will I feel, thinking all these horrible things if it turns out that's what happened? How? I know how. Here's the worst, Friend. Here's something to frown at. One more horrible thought on top of all my others. I would—yes, I would rather know they had an accident than think Ken is up there with Marge and Burt, all three of them drunk, Marge and Burt sitting there laughing at Ken because he's passed out and they're wondering how to get him home, laughing, having another drink, feeling no pain like

Pain coming up to punish me—for such an evil wish—like wishing the—oh, Friend—wish the pain wouldn't come! No more—no more, no—more—please! Trying to let it —trying to stay loose—let it go—go—going. Maybe I should be pushing? I wish I knew. I wish Ken would come. I wish it was over. I wish I was never pregnant.

I wish I had never met Ken, I wish—the worst wish of all is already wished, that Ken has had an accident instead of what I know happened. Instead of being gone when I need him the most. Letting me down. Maybe I'll die and then all that won't matter. But if I live, what will it be like when I see him again? What will he say to me? What will I say? Nothing. I never want to see him again. I'll sell the land and take the money and my baby and I'll go—where can I go? I could go back to Mom and Dad. They want my money too so I could go home and give the money to Dad and they'd let me stay and—no, I could never go back there. That would be worse than—I could take my money and go back to Berkeley and Evelyn and I could get an apartment together. We used to talk about that, about putting our money together to hire some girl to help us do what we couldn't. *Better than marrying one of these damned partials or some screwed-up man who wants to take care of a little helpless blind woman. They the worst! No! We'll be lovers, you and me, forget all those men!* But Evelyn's dead. I forgot. I must be losing my mind. She's dead. Friend, don't let me lose my mind too. Calm. Calm. Evelyn's dead. No friends but you, Friend. So I'll live alone with the baby, hire some help. Where? In Berkeley? Can't go back there. Berkeley is a one-time place. San Jose? No one there I know anymore. I've changed too much. Too close to Mom and Dad. San Francisco. I could start all over, just me and the baby and—I don't want to go there! I don't want to go to any city anywhere. I like it here. I love it. It's my first real home. It's where I belong, I knew the first time we came here that it was my home. But it'll be different now. Because everything between Ken and me will be different. Can't ever be the same again. Not after this. Even if I don't die and the baby doesn't die, something else dies, something between Ken and me. Now I understand what Maggie said when I asked her why she had never been married. I thought she'd say it was because her artist lover died. I was wrong. *Oh, my dear, I couldn't, I'm much too selfish. You see, in every marriage I've ever known . . . now I'm only talking about the few good ones! In every marriage, there's a beautiful start. For a while we make it perfect, make it all truth and love. For a few years, maybe three or five or seven. And then . . . something happens. Has to. A betrayal, my dear, inevitable as rain, because it is part of the separateness of human beings, the flaw. Whatever happens isn't the important thing. It's the failure of understanding by someone you thought, with all his weaknesses, knew you so well that he couldn't possibly do that one thing that—well, those are the good marriages and they don't break up. They go on. But they're not the same. And, selfish fool that I am, I had to have all or nothing. So that's what I've had several times. All. And then nothing.* Then why was she so happy that Ken and I were getting married? *You're the exceptions, you two. Your weaknesses are right out in the open. You know each other's handicaps and you're not such fools as to . . .* but she was wrong. What she said, it happened to us even though I knew about Ken's problem. And it didn't happen after three years or five. We didn't even get one year. And our marriage will be like all the others Maggie has known . . . something dead in it. Because I love this land and I haven't anywhere else to go and I guess I will still love Ken in a way if I live and the baby lives. But it won't be the same anymore. We'll go on and on and after a while I won't think very often of how he let me down and I'll even tell myself I've forgotten it though I won't, can't ever forget it but after years and years I won't remember that things were ever any different between us years and years ago when our love was whole. Years and years . . . all the years and years coming. They make me tired. Make me wish I could just sleep, sleep away all the

Here it comes. Pretend I'm asleep. Going to sleep through this one, foetal position, me and the baby both—sleeping! Stay loose—loosen arms—loosen legs—no—more. More? Filling—filling me! Through the blood—down to my toes—up—top of head—out—out—loose! But I can't—going—going. Will they get stronger than that? I couldn't stand it stronger than that. I thought it would hurt just in my stomach, between my legs, but it only starts there. It starts like a drop of water in my stomach but then it grows and swells like water heated to steam, it grows outward through my back, down my legs, out my arms, up my chest, neck, to my eyes, to my brain, until I'm filled up with pain, I'm nothing but a skin stretched tight over pain. And then it slowly, slowly shrinks again, goes back down, down to that little drop. And the drop disappears too. Nothing. No pain. Unbelievable. Where does it go? How could it have grown so huge? I must have imagined it. Crazy. Pain like that makes you crazy, blots out the brain. Impossible. But real. And it will come back. Soon the pain will last as long as the time between the pains. All the books said that. One minute pain, one minute rest. Rest? One minute waiting, not resting, waiting with another kind of pain, the knowing that the pain will come again. And always stronger. Much worse than it is now. Friend, is this the way it is supposed to be? Is this the way it always is? Is that why the Bible had to call it a punishment from God? How else explain anything so hard? What a mean god. I'm glad I don't believe in god or I'd hate him. Only you, Friend, I believe in you. But what help are you? You just listen. You care. A lot of good that does. Is this the way everyone gets born? All the billions of people? Nothing Ken read to me sounded like this. *Very strong contractions.* Those words don't have anything to do with this. Maybe this isn't the way it's supposed to be. Maybe something is wrong. Am I bleeding? All this wet, smells like water, no smell of blood. But is this normal? Maybe not. Maybe everything was all right until now, the way the doctor said, but now it's not right. Too early, three weeks early. Not normal labor? Baby stuck somehow? And this will just go on and on until my mind and my body drain out in screams and blood and I die. That's what used to happen when women lived on farms and had their babies at home. The old graveyard at the other end of town, stones from before 1900, we walked through there and saw the dates, young women buried with their dead babies. The baby would die too? I guess so. Do I care? Yes. No. I'm not thinking of the baby at all. I don't feel there's a baby in me. There's just this pain, sleeping now but waking up soon to—no, I won't think about it, won't think about pain, won't think about dying. I can't even if I tried. Can't imagine dying. Dying. Dead. Dead. Saying the word doesn't make it more real. Imagine not being. No. I can't. That's like imagining not imagining. Like trying to imagine nothing. Nothing. I used to do that when I was little, try to imagine what that word meant. Try to imagine . . . nothing. In my mind I would try to take the whole universe and squeeze it down, down, down to . . . nothing. But then there would be all that space outside, all around where I'd squeezed it down so I'd know I hadn't done it, couldn't do it, couldn't grab it all and squeeze it down because there'd be something, me squeezing, the space all around . . . there'd always be something, there couldn't be any such thing as nothing. Does that mean dying isn't . . . stop thinking about dying. Think about the music, listen to the music. It's almost at the end and I don't think I can get up to change the tape, so this is the last music I'll hear until . . . maybe the last music I'll ever—stop those thoughts. Listen. Beautiful at the end after all Psyche's sufferings are over, all tasks done. All. She has been to Hades and come back again, she's been lifted up by Eros, lifted up, how does the chorus sing it? Soaring to the light . . . miracle of love. And then the music climbs and climbs and soars and then sinks, so peaceful, so quiet, an ending of such peace. Peace like sleep? No, deeper. Like death? No. A complete peace that is like

Friend!

It's coming. Friend, hold me, help me so I can let go while you—hold—me. Not fighting it—no—I'm not—not no, say yes—yes. Yes doesn't help—doesn't—hurts—hurts whatever I—HURTS! There. Letting go. Let me go. Not fighting it . . . that doesn't help the pain. But it saves energy, that book said, energy I'll need at the end for pushing. The end? When is that? Those books scare me now. Liars. All those calm things they say. *Save energy. Strong contractions.* All those words that say but don't say what's going to happen. I should have been suspicious when Ken read the one that said *don't panic.* Oh, tired. I'm already so tired and nowhere near. . .and cold. The fire. Can't let it go out. Get up and build it up again. Can I? Yes, I can stand. I can walk. Pile on the wood. Feel that? Fire flaring up, feel it, warm? Hot. But doesn't warm me, not inside. Have to pee. Outhouse? No, I can't walk that far. Just outside the door, quick, open, close. Squat, hang on to the door, rain will wash it all away. Easy. Calm. Don't worry, another minute or two before the next pain. And between pains I'm still strong. Quieter out here. Rain falling gently, gently, sinking soft into the earth. Not like being in the house with that tin roof rattle. Don't stay out here, too cold. Lonely. Lonelier out in all this space, quiet rain. Get inside, shut the door. Roof rattle, rattle, rattle! No use putting on more music, couldn't hear it anymore with that rattle so hard and steady. A new roof, shingles, Ken promised for next year. If there is a next year for me. Tired, Friend, awfully tired. Yes, you already know. Thirsty. Sip of water. Good, that's very good. Another sip then back to bed, back to bed. Wet. Wiggle over to the other side, near the wall, Ken's side where it's still dry. But cold. Warm up the bed, Friend, send me warm thoughts to warm up the bed. That's right, we'll take a nice little rest, pretend to sleep again, just for a few seconds, pain starting again any second now but rest, rest. Close our eyes. We won't think about the next pain, about the time. Make me forget, Friend, so I just rest. If you could do me this favor . . . I've been good, I haven't asked you . . . maybe a little time to think, to rest, before the next pain. Wouldn't that be nice! You and I could just talk a little together, think a little, no more complaints, I promise, just pass the time together listening to the rain rattle the roof, listening to the music. Didn't the music end? No, there's more to

PSYCHE, more and more, a new part of the music I never heard before. You've been saving that for me? A special part, slow and stately with a sweet melody, sweet like a song a child would sing. But sad. Oh, what a sad, beautiful melody. Sung by a child, all innocent, happy. But sad too? Sad. The grownup inside the singing child knows what the child doesn't know, knows that pain is coming. So inside at the very center, the song is sad and the child whistles little fancy turns all around the sad notes. Her whistling dances all around the melody. Have you ever seen a dancing whistle? You're hearing one now, Friend. With such energy. On and on. Never heard music like that. Just listen . . . beautiful . . . as . . . as a . . . feel how it touches everything. . . turns everything into a dancing whistle. Dancing. Dancing. Rain dancing on the roof. Millions of drops stamping and jumping and falling and leaping. While the fire dances, leaps up to it, crack, crack, spit, sizz. Wild dances to the sweet sad song, whistling happy song, sweet and sad. Making everything dance. Rain and fire dancing to something else in the song, something the rain hears, something the fire hears. And I too. I dance. Flying up to the ceiling to join the stamping of the rain drops, bouncing up from the bed, light, light as air, see how I leap up. And float. Float down so slowly my toe barely touches the floor before I leap, float up again like dancing on the moon, dancing between fire and water, a flying, floating dance that you taught me, Friend. And you are so pleased, so proud of my dance! Proud as the rain and the fire. Proud as the sweet melody, growing sweeter and higher and purer than any music I ever heard. Is what I hear music? Is what I hear . . . hearing at all? Or something behind sound, behind music, in music, the center of music, the meaning beyond sound. I knew it was there! I must tell everyone, it's true, it exists, the meaning beyond sound! I must dance it. If I stop dancing, it will stop, disappear. I float in front of the fire and the music stops, the raindrops stop dancing, the fire glows but does not dance. Everything is still. I am still. We are in the silence in the center of the music. Waiting. Waiting as the door . . . slowly . . . opens. Ken! Oh, Ken, you did come back. Ken, the baby is coming. You smile. I've never seen you smile so happily. Yes, I'm happy too. There's still time, just time to get to the hospital. No, don't worry, I'm fine. It doesn't hurt at all now. I remember some hurting, but that's all gone. It's not going to hurt anymore because you're here and I'm not afraid and we can—you keep smiling and smiling as if you have a happy secret. What is your secret? What's happening behind the door? Why didn't you close it? Is someone else there? Maggie? Oh, Maggie, you've come back too and you look so young, tiny and golden with hummingbird wings and a silver wand, the magic wand you wave over us to grant all our wishes. More? Who else? Is that what took you so long? You brought everyone! A surprise party to celebrate the baby's coming. *I've just written a forty-hour poem, an ode to new life!* Yes, everyone, let Madeline stand here near the fire to read her poem . . . whistle her poem? Yes, a new kind of poem that you whistle instead of—but Davide is trying to drown you out. Davide is reading a letter. He wears a brown cassock and he is bending low to carry the cross on his back. Oh, his voice is so loud, so deep, shouting his letter in deep words, held out long, long. His voice comes out so loud, like a deep, long moan. *Dear God!* Quiet everyone, let's hear

Davide's letter. That's all right, Madeline, you can go on whistling your poem but everyone else, quiet, I want to hear this. Everyone, all you people from the Homer Center, quiet. I want to hear your letter to God, Davide, because I always wanted to write a letter to God. So did everyone else, didn't we all? Look, they pretend not to care, not to be listening. Talking. Laughing. Pretending they don't care, pretending you're crazy to write to God when all the time they want to write to God too. But don't know how to start or what to say. *Dear God!* Yes, Davide, go on. But not so loud. You moan so loud, I can't make out a word, not a word of it. Can you, Ken? Oh, make Davide stop moaning. *That's not Davide, it's Mr. Canfield.* Oh dear, he's reading his list of handicapped geniuses again. But those aren't famous names . . . what names are . . . oh, he's reading the names of students at the Homer Center. All handicapped geniuses! Everyone of us! How proud they are! Yes, that's it, each take a bow as Mr. Canfield reads your name. We are all . . . all handicapped geniuses. And I take a bow too, and I'm so glad I wore my wedding dress. *Splendid, my dear.* Maggie waves her wand. *Like a young goddess!* A lovely party, a great party for the baby when it's born . . . or was it already born? I forget. Ken? Has our baby come? *Not yet, Lon. Soon. But Lon, let's not have it born here at the Med.* Oh no, we mustn't. Too dark in the Med. Dark inside with all these people and that black river rushing by outside, people floating by, sinking, drowning in it, but hot in here and crowded, and the hiss of steam coming up from all these cracks in the rock, the black hard rock, oh, be careful where you walk, don't fall through one of those great cracks or . . . hold my hand, Ken. Ken? Not here? But he brought me in . . . left me? Left me again? Where's Ken? Davide. Madeline. Stop crying and moaning! Listen to me! How do I find Ken . . . where has he . . . listen! *I'm listening.* Evelyn! Oh, Evelyn, I never hoped to see you again. Help me, Evelyn, help me find Ken. Tell me what to do. *Get out of here, girl!* Yes, but where do I go? Where's Ken? *Not that way, not out into that black river, that's poison. This way, out the back. See the tunnel?* Yes, yes, I see it. *Well, run!* I'm going. I'm running. Moaning, they're all moaning and calling me. *Don't listen, girl, run!* Yes. Run. Won't listen. Running. Climbing. Ken, I'm coming. Wait for me. Fast as I can. Uphill. Steps. Rocks. Up. Why is it always uphill? Out of breath. Keep running. Climb. Crawl. Legs move slowly, dragging, pulling. Running again. Reaching legs way . . . up . . . and . . . out. To run. But so slow. Can't. Can't. Must! Look ahead. Lighter. Up ahead there's light. End of the tunnel. Coming, I'm coming, Ken, running, but so slow, so tired, so sleepy. To the light. Ken. Ken, I see you! I'm coming. I'm trying. Oh, Ken, I can't. My legs won't . . . see how they move so . . . oh, catch me, I'm falling, falling asleep. Falling. Into your arms! Oh, Ken, it's going to be all right now. I got back all right. I found you. You were waiting all the time, weren't you? *Yes, Lon. Let's go.* Where? Where are you taking me? Lifting me, carrying me up, up, floating up to . . . home! Home. High up here on the slope. Feel the warm sun coming up behind us, lighting up everything. Look down on the meadow, the creek, oh, how beautiful it is, and how we've made it bloom! Trees and flowers and silvery grass and bright fruit hanging off the trees, silvery grass singing, hear it sing? Oh, Ken, how you smile, how beautiful to see you smile so peacefully, how good it is to see . . . to see? To see! Ken, it's a miracle, isn't it? I can see you. Just the way I knew you would look, with golden curls like Maggie said, with silver streaks, and bright eyes in a wise face so full of love, strong love. Such a sweet smile, as sweet as the music I was dancing to. Did you hear it? Gone now. Hold me, Ken. Arms around me. Hold me while we look at our garden lighting up, dawn rising over all of it, while you hold me tight. No. Not so tight. Ken. Ken! Too tight. Ken, you're hurting me! Don't squeeze so tight. No, it hurts! Hurts! Please Ken, DON'T

HURT ME! Don't . . . no. Oh, no. Ken. No. No Ken. A dream. A dream. No Ken. No Davide moaning. That was me. No dawn. No miracle. If dawn comes, I won't see it. I slept. How long? What time? Four. The pains stopped for a while and I slept. Now starting again. Harder. Oh, Ken, why—no, I won't cry. Why not! Cry! I can't hold back crying anymore. He's not coming. Oh, Friend, such a cruel dream. Yes, I know I asked for rest, but to have a dream like that and then wake up alone . . . dark . . . still. Even the rain has stopped. Everything has stopped. Everything but . . . why shouldn't I cry. And sob. And yell. *Save energy,* say the books. Fuck the books. Make all the noise I want. Cry like a baby, howling, blubbering, drooling and, yes, go ahead and let that screech come up my throat, up and out. I don't care what noise I make. No one to hear me. Doesn't matter. No reason to be brave. Friend won't even hear me, not even watching now, invisible Friend dissolving in my tears. Cry. The way that woman in that newsreel cried over her baby's body. For the first time cry without anyone here to tell me to stop, without me telling myself to stop. Cry for . . . for everything. Because it hurts. Because I'm afraid. Because Ken isn't coming, has left me alone. Because I can never love him now, not the way I thought I would learn to. Because I'm going to die. The baby too. Because it doesn't matter if I die. Because the best woman I ever knew is dead. Because life is a waste and people get all twisted and mangled and broken in it. Like Davide and Madeline and . . . like all those sick people huddling in the gutter on Telegraph mumbling *change* and never will change because they're broken. Like me. Me. Because I'm blind, blind, blind. Can't read a book, can't see people and sky and birds and trees. Blind is ugly. Ugly. In the streets people backed off, pulling their children away, shadows shrinking away from the ugly blind. As if not seeing wasn't bad enough there were all those people who wished I wasn't there, wished they could be blind to me, like the waiters in the restaurants, like the friends from high school who didn't want to be bothered, like Mom and Dad who wished I would disappear and wanted to disappear themselves, escape, run away. But I was the one who ran away to this place, a place to die, a place where no one has made good from the beginning, jinxed, cursed, not the paradise I tried to see in my head, in my head, because I couldn't see it as it really is. So now there'll be a new story to tell about this place where the poor blind girl died . . . alone . . . screaming. Died the way people all over the world are dying of starvation or of torture or of slave labor or of boredom or of the radiation drifting over them on the wind, all the dying people all over the world who can't even comfort each other because they can't love or care or let themselves feel a thing because if they do they'll cry the way I am crying, cry their lives away from knowing and caring and feeling all the pain, the pain, the

Pain.

Back—pressing back. Swelling up my back—up in a wave—huge wave—sweeps me up—takes all of me—up—till I—am—PAIN—pain—less—less—leaving now—back? It leaves a backache. Going. No, backache stays. Strong . . . aching . . . breaking back. That one came closer. How long? Ken was going to time—forget Ken, forget timing pains. What does it matter how long—go ahead and cry. No? No tears. Maybe no one can cry hard, hard like that for very long. Have I cried out my whole life in a couple of minutes? No. I suppose there's plenty of time for more crying. If I want to. Don't. Done crying. Listen, Friend, you know how it's going to be. You knew all along and didn't tell me because I wasn't ready to know. All right. All right. So I'm going to have my baby alone. No one is going to rescue me at the last minute. No one is going to tell me what to do, how to do it. I might die. I might not. Either way, this could go on for a long time. The first baby takes time, the books said, maybe even hours after the pains get close. I can't TAKE hours of—don't think about it. I won't think of hours, of time. Just think of one pain at a time. Live one pain at a time until—but I'm not ready. There must be things to get ready, and I'm still curled up in this clammy wet bed! But I can't move. When a pain comes I can't even think. Sure, but that's only when a pain comes. Between pains I have time to do things to get ready. What has to be done? I can't think—yes I can! No one else will think for me. No time to say I can't think. No time to be afraid. No time to be mad at Ken or at anyone else. No time to hold a funeral for every sad life or death. Soon the time between pains will be only resting, resting, when I can't move, can't think. But right now there is time, and I'm all right. See, I can get up, sit on the edge of the bed, sit up straight, one hand holding back . . . pushing against backache, does that help? Between pains I can do what I need to do to get ready. If I keep my head. If I don't get scared and waste time thinking how awful the pain was or how much worse the next one is going to be. No time to waste being scared. No matter how hard the pains come, they're just pains. A pain is a pain. Nothing else. Awful, but not to be afraid of. No good to be afraid or hate it or wish it wouldn't come. The pain is the pain and it comes and then it goes. When it goes I have to be ready to do something, to think fast and do fast before the next one comes. Where do I start? What should I get ready first? Something to cut the cord with? How? What should I put near the bed for when I can't get up anymore? The bed? I'll have to change it, all wet. I can't lie down again in all those wet, clammy sheets. More sheets in one of the boxes, all nearly labeled in Braille. Right after the next pain, I'll get up and . . . yes, getting tight, starting in my back again. Now, don't worry, just

Just let—let loose—sit easy—calm—think about—plan—plan what? No, can't—can't think—CAN—LOOSE—don't let it take me—there—when it—going now—when I get to—the top, can't think anymore, thoughts pushed out, pain fills up my brain.

Only for a few seconds. Remember that. It comes, but it goes. Then time to think, plan, do something. Now, quick, before the next one. On your feet. Can I? Sure. Up easy. The fire. First the fire. Mustn't go out, must keep the place warm, first need of mother and baby, right? Build it up high, higher. Wood box getting low, can't bend to get those—yes, side bend, bend sideways and pick up those last pieces. But that means I'll have to go outside to the woodpile and get more wood. All right. Put that on list of things to do between pains. Should have done it earlier when I could —no thinking about should-have-done. You can do it. Woodpile against the house under the overhang, dry, even after rain. No more rain. No rattle on the roof, only a few thumps of water falling from tree branches. Silence. Can hear myself think, plan. First the wood, then—no, better not go now, not enough time before the next pain. Wait and plan. After next pain get the wood, after another pain change the bed. After . . . go back to bed now to wait? No, don't even want to sit on that cold, wet . . . thirsty. Enough time for a drink. Hungry too? When did I have that apple? A million years ago. Water first, a tall glass of water, the best water I ever tasted, through brand new pipes from our lovely, clear spring. Lips so dry, throat too. Best drink I ever tasted. Now what's left to eat? An orange. Can I peel it in time? How long does it take to peel, rip, tear . . . hands shaking. Quiet. Easy. Sit down, slowly . . . carefully . . . lower-down easy. My back will break if I sit down hard. Easy. There. Sitting. Leaking water won't hurt a wooden chair. Peel. Face the window. Dark. Dark as can be. Maybe there are stars out there now that the rain is over. Maybe the sky is even getting lighter . . . no, not yet, dawn comes late this time of year. From now on everything gets darker and darker . . . oh, that's the best taste in the world. So sweet. Hurry. Stop shaking. But my legs are so cold. Should have got my blanket. No, don't get up to get it. No time. How long does it take to eat an orange? Hurry now before the next pain . . . eat and plan, after the next one I'll—is it starting—must be—no, not a—it's coming up again. After all that trouble, using up a whole time between pains to peel and eat, stuffing the whole orange down, now am I going to—going to be sick. Going to throw up! Quick. Hand over mouth. Sink? Where? Where am I? All turned around. Grab. Wall. Wall! Door. Pull open the door! Quick, swing—open—out—outside—out—out—OUT! It all came up. All my precious orange, my sweet—oh no, here comes

Hold
on. To what? It's coming up—up—try to relax—feet apart—steady. Brace yourself against the house—support—easy—won't fall—no—won't—pain shaking the house! No, just legs shaking—steady now, it's going—going. Starting again? Not in my back now. Stomach. Could be another pain? No, not so soon. Bowels. Outhouse. Have to go—no, not enough time, waste of time. I might stumble on the way if a pain comes. No, I have to do it here. Here? Right outside the door? No, around the corner, in the dirt, add my mud to the mud the rain made. Scoop out a little hole here right next to the house. Crouch over the hole, lean back against the house. There, that's steady, feels good to my back. I won't fall. I'm okay. Diarrhea. Like water. Vomitting and diarrhea, water coming out of both ends. That's all right. Normal. Books said

so. At the hospital they give you an enema. No room for anything inside. No food. Better not even drink any more water. Or just a little bit. Just sips when my mouth gets dry. But inside my body, there's nothing going on anymore but this baby pushing out. No, the baby's not pushing. Being pushed. By my body that can't do anything but push. That's the pain, pushing down on the baby. Does it hurt the baby too? Does it push and squeeze it? And the baby feels the water leaking away, like out of a bathtub, and it's bumping against hard sides that move in from all around . . . and squeeze! Is the baby afraid? Doesn't want to come out. Yes, Baby. It's cold out here and very hard and often sad. I don't blame you for not wanting to come out here to live. I don't think I would want to either. Probably I never wanted to even after I was out and had forgotten what it was like to just float. No thinking, no getting hurt or scared inside there. No having to do things, decide, learn things you wished you didn't know, thinking for a while that someone can protect you even outside and then learning that you're really all alone and—but still . . . it's beautiful here outside. Even blind, it's beautiful. After a rain when everything is washed clean and it's so quiet I feel the whole world listening, even the invisible stars way out there . . . listening too. Everything alive and listening to the water soaking into the earth, sinking down deep into the world. All the trees and the grass drenched and washed, the water pouring off still, in little rivers running down the branches, or clinging to the leaves and then letting go, drop, thud, drip, plop, a hundred different soft tones splashing green smells. Breathe. Oh, Friend, just breathe in those wonderful green smells. I wish I could stay out here. I wish I could have my baby out here, on the earth, with the green smells and the soft splashes and the stars watching. You're bigger out here too, Friend, closer. But . . . no. Too cold. Too wet. Am I empty? Yes. Better get up and—oh no, I think it's too late. Better wait . . . don't move until

Back firm against the wall—don't tense—no fear—just pain. Take the pain here as well as—loose arms—oh—stars? Friend? Loose—hang head loose—there. Going down . . . down . . . less. Get up? No. Not too soon. Wait a little, make sure it's all gone. Almost. Never all gone in my back. That wasn't so bad. Brace myself to get up. Not bad. It felt . . . better, like when I was sitting at the table. It feels better when I'm not lying down. When I go back to bed I'll sit up. There. Standing. Cold. Oh, I'm cold. Legs freezing. Got to get warm. Stop shaking, get inside. Wait, first the wood. Around the side of the house. But what can I carry, how many trips and getting cold every time I come out. Have to get warm and stay warm. If I could just get one of those big logs, it would burn for a couple of hours, then smolder, coals, ashes giving heat, and by then the sun will be up to warm the house. Big logs. Ken put them—yes, here on the side. Heavy? Too heavy. I can carry one, but just barely, and Ken never let me because of the baby, never carry anything heavy, lose the baby. But does it matter now? Baby's coming anyway. No, careful, everything inside is pushing and straining enough without—oh, Friend, if you could just lift the other end of this. I can drag it! Take this end and pull. Is that too hard? No, not bad, just a few inches at a time. Pull. Rest. Pull. Easy. Don't rush. Still plenty of time. Pull. Old dead tree. Pull. Ken selected so carefully what to burn. Pull. *Not going to ruin this place. When we die, Lon, let's leave it better for our children.* Pull. He cut up that huge old tree, chopping every morning for an hour. Pull. A whole month to get it down to little pieces, with a few big logs like this. Pull. Easier here on the porch. Pull. No strain. Door must be—right here. Open. Oh, nice warm air in there. Pull. Don't get stuck in the doorway. Easy. Pull easy. Nothing's going to happen if you leave the door open a minute. And if the pain comes? Well, then I'll just sit down in the doorway on the log until it passes, then get up and pull again. Pull. Inside. Shut the door. Pull. No, just drop it, roll it. Over to the fireplace. Suppose it's too big—no worry, Ken measured every cut to make sure. It...roll...will be...roll...just right. Now roll it up onto the hearth. Need to lift it now, just one end, then slant it over, half into the fire. Half out! If I can't get it all in, it'll start to burn and burn the house down and—save your imagination! Ugh, smoke, lift, push, just a little...there! There. All right? Yes, all right. Didn't hurt myself, don't feel sick, not hurt, everything fine. A good fire that will last for hours. Now the bed. No. Take it easy. Sit right down here and rest. Face the fire, just sit easy and wait for the next pain. Not afraid. Just ready. Just rest and wait. No waiting.

Just in time. Starting. Watch the fire. See? Little streak of flame—bit of light—concentrate—light—streak—bright little—hold the fire—hold it in my eyes—hold—oh no, don't lose—Friend, help me! Yes. That was the top. Loose. Down...all...the...way. Fire. Down. That's it. That's better. All over, and not too bad, watching the fire, holding that little glow like tiny lightning streaks breaking my darkness. Hope I never lose that much, that bit of light. Concentrate on it. Like hypnotism. It does help. I wish...too bad I can't move the bed so I could be right in front of the fire. No wishes. Get busy, just enough time to change the sheets and get back to bed. Get up...easy...there. Pull off those wet sheets and—oh, the mattress is soaked. Wet. Cold. How could I still be leaking after losing so much water? Won't be any left to help the baby out. *Dry birth.* Once an old lady was telling my mother about—don't think about that. Make the bed. But what's the use. I'd just shiver in it, cold and wet. Maybe I could make a bed by the fire. Pull blankets off, put them on the floor, pull off the quilt too, lay them all out in front, this way, so I can face the fire, watching the light when the pain comes. Try that. Lie down. There, that's—no, too hard, too flat. My back! Oh, flat and hard that way makes my back hurt! Can't raise my head, can't see the fire. No good. Floor cold even through the blankets, need more on the floor. Start again. Newspapers. I won't need them anymore for the fire. Spread newspapers, like old men in the park, layers of newspapers, warm, insulation, soak up the water...the blood? How much blood? Don't think about that. Now something I can lean against. Another log from outside? No. Something slanting. Don't have anything. Ages ago women had birth chairs. Chair no good. Chair. Think. This wooden chair, pull forward, turn it over, upside down, chair legs pointing up in the air. Now the back slants from the floor up! But I can't lie on newspapers. Not clean. The quilt again, the blankets, all blankets off the bed. Don't hurry. There's still time. Out of breath, slow down, easy, breathe easy. Now, pillows on my backrest, all pillows. Good. Then something waterproof. Tom's rain parka. Where did I—here on the sink. Dry now? Dry. Spread out where my bottom touches the floor, just below the chair back. Something over that. A sheet. Sheets and towels packed in that low box. Here. Sheets and towels, nice little Braille label. Drag the whole box near the fire. I'll need more sheets, maybe towels later. Spread sheet, folded. Just one sheet? One at a time, I can change it when it gets wet. Oh, my back—starting again? Not just yet. Now, I'll try it, just lower myself down to the floor, back against the chair back, old broken chair, will it snap when I lean back? No, fine, just fine. Rest back, let my weight go back. It's all right. Feels good against my back, and I can see the fire. Bright and hot, warming me up. Out of breath. Easy. It's starting. Rest and watch the fire. Comfortable. Easy. Watch. Here we go.

Think about—watch light, dancing light—think about—what next? Things to keep near—oh, already up to my neck—no more—more? Head—eyes—think? Can't! Watch the fire—more—so—long? No more room for—no more! Friend! Loose—stay loose—doesn't help—nothing helps! How can a minute...be...so...long? Going. That doctor. *The pains never last more than a minute.* One minute. Sounded like no time at all. He never said how long a minute can be. I have to remember to watch the fire but stay loose. So hard...to concentrate and relax at the same time. But if I don't...at the top I'm hanging on by a thread and if I let go, I'll—don't think about it. One pain at a time. Do something. What? What else do I need here? Thirsty. No, don't drink, I'll just throw up. Just a little? A tiny glass of water next to me, just to wet my mouth, just a little sip. Roll over, get up. Okay, where's that little tin cup, measuring cup, so if I knock it over I won't have broken glass all over. Half full, put it down on the floor, on my right. What else? I'm cold with nothing on but Ken's wool shirt. Legs still get cold. But everything gets wet if I—socks, those long wool socks Ken wore with the hip boots, fishing socks. Where? He packed them. In a suitcase? This one is baby clothes, this one is my stuff. Rucksack? Feel them? No. What's this—oh, just pull everything out, don't worry about—here! Good, scratchy, thick, wool, and long! Sit down on the other chair and pull them on. Good idea, but how to reach my toes over this great belly. Squiggle feet up, around, seems harder than ever because of where the baby has dropped to. Soon, no belly. Soon all this will be over. Soon. There, socks all the way up my thighs. Warm. What else do I need? The cord. You tie strings in two places, then cut between. In that book on home birth, which we decided against, no home birth for me! A knife and string. Dirty knife. I can put it into the fire to clean it just before—which knife out of the drawer in the sink? The big one? How thick is the cord? Oh, the paring knife will do, it's sharper than—what am I laughing at? Giggling. Look at me, Friend, I'm hysterical. Stop. Please stop. Try to stop laughing. Me holding a little knife and talking about cutting the cord. I may die and all I can think about is that cord, like if I don't cut it I'll go through the rest of my life with my baby attached to me, like cutting that cord is the only thing I have to worry about. I can see this knife just cutting into it like—no, I couldn't. No. Here's the knife, here's the string. Put them down all neat beside my cup of water. But I know I won't use them. Cut into flesh, my flesh, the baby's? Both together. Our flesh. Cut into our flesh? No, I'll never be able to do it. Never be able to do any of this. Tired. Lean back. Rest. So tired. Almost could fall asleep again. Limp. Don't think I can get up again, not for

Keep eyes closed. Rest while it starts. Not too bad yet. Stay limp and loose. But I'm tired and—not ready yet, not—eyes open! Watch the flame—watch—hang on—let go but hang onto—the fire—blaze—glare—flame—no! Don't say no—no hurts—makes more—pain! Stronger than—can't say yes—then don't say anything. Anything. Going now. Let eyes close again. Rest and feel the pain shrinking. Lovely. Delicious. Better than no pain, that feeling of the pain shrinking. Rest. I could sleep. Don't want to move again. Except to fight that pain, fight it off? No use to fight, the pain is stronger than I am, but I want to get it. . . out. No room in me for that much pain. Want to push that pain out. Too big to. . . is it time to push? Can't think. Going to sleep now, sleep. My mind is limp, wet, foggy wet limp, squeezed out rag. Think. Is everything ready? Wake up and think, just in case there is something else to get ready. I might not be able to get up again. Last chance. Am I ready? How do I know? Never did this before, how do I know what to do? I'm not doing it, something else is doing it, that pain inside is doing it, swelling up until it gets so big that I'll burst and—stop feeling sorry for yourself and think. Anything else I can get ready? For me. For the baby. The baby. I forgot all about it. When the baby comes out, what will it need? Clothes? Water to bathe it? There's only cold water. No, cold water would be bad. Something to wrap it in? where are the baby clothes, the hospital suitcase, Maggie's suitcase. Get up, easy, I can get up once more. Dizzy. Hold on to the leg of the chair, careful, don't tip it over. Easy, I'm steady, I can walk a few steps to the boxes, find that nice, smooth case, the one that was going to the hospital. Didn't I put it right on top of the table? Just a few hours ago? Seems like ages ago. Yes, here, right on top. Full of all the things to take to the hospital. Lacy nightgown, satin slippers, hand lotion, two new Braille books, two head scarves, all presents from Maggie. Don't need them now, no satin slippers for this birth, no—never mind, where are the baby clothes? Here, diaper, shirt, wrapper, booties, hat, oh, and this huge, soft cotton shawl from Spain. Woven by some old woman so many years ago. Maggie brought it back from Spain. *Precious to me, my dear, full of sad memories, but fine, brave memories too. I want you to have it for the baby.* Whatever was precious to her, she gave to me. Because I was more precious to her. I am. I hope she's all right. I hope nothing happened to her. I'll use this, Maggie's shawl, hang it over the sticking-up chair leg, near me, near the fire, hanging there and getting warm so that when the baby comes out I can reach back and get the shawl and wrap it up all soft, warm. Now. Lower myself. . .down. . .easy. This is the last time. There. Settled. Can I reach the cup? The knife and string? Box of towels. And reach back, can I reach the shawl? Have I done it all, Friend? Whatever else there is to do, I don't know, so it won't be done and I couldn't get up again now to do anything. Tired. Too tired. And I have to rest before the next

Oh, it's already here. Couldn't it give me a minute—a few more seconds—how boring for it to keep coming back like—loose. Stay loose? No! No, I want this out—out—push this pain out! Push? Is it time to—doctor said he would tell me when to start. No doctor—no one to tell me—when—how? Like a bowel movement? No—push—all of me—bowels and all—push—out of breath—can't breathe and push—can't. Try. Can't do what I don't know how to do—going. Pain going. I'm crying. Not crying, just tears. Never mind. How can I learn how to do something I've never done? Against all I've ever—all my life, closing, protecting the opening of my body. Even when making love, holding Ken, holding. That's not pushing, that's holding and squeezing and taking him in to me. I never learned to push like this and after I knew I was pregnant I couldn't practice because I might lose the baby. No time in my life is this kind of pushing any good. Never, never must do it. Until now, all at once, I have to do it, learn to do it. Tired. That made me tired. How many times do I have to do that before it's over? That's why women die. Forget that. Rest and think. Think. Next time, when it starts, I'll take a deep breath, deep. Can I take enough in to hold it for a minute? A minute doesn't seem so long to hold my breath. A minute of pain lasts forever. Never mind. I'll take a deep, deep breath when the pain starts. Takes a few seconds to do that, so it's not a whole minute I have to hold it. Then, when I'm full of air, start to push. How? Any old way. Important thing is to hold my breath, can't breathe or I lose the push and then the pain sinks back into me... fills me to—don't think about that. Rest. Close my eyes. Just go right off to sleep. Limp. Think about things that make me happy and peaceful, happy dreams, just like going into a deep long sleep, hours and hours asleep with

A wave crashing! Gush! The roof broke? Water fell in? No. No. Me! Water all over. Fire sizzling. Water spurted out of me all the way to the fire. Oh no, did I put out the fire? Giggling, hysterical, but it's so funny and awful if I put the fire out. No, I see streaks, the flame streaks. Water only hit some coals. Smokey smell. Water all over, broken like an ocean wave. How could I have so much water left in me? Pain rising fast. Take a deep breath. More, deep. Can't get more, have to push. Is this right? Push hard! Can't. Breath gone, gone—gone at—the top—top—pain's going back into me! No! Gasp, push, gasp, push. Oh, that's not right. Push. Forget it! Going. Going. Rest while it goes, sinks, shrinks away. Rest in a puddle, water splashed clear to the fire. Ocean wave. I am an ocean. And I didn't feel it at all. As if the water flew out of nowhere. Crashing, splashing. And that wasn't a good push. Can't I take a breath and hold it just like swimming under water? But to take a breath and hold it and push like that—can't do it, breath all comes out, gets used up. Not like swimming or—not like anything. Has to be steady. Hard. Not a quick push, like pushing once, there, it's all over. No, a long, long time holding the push. Bearing down. That's what someone called it. Mom? Bearing down. A steady holding, opening out, forcing, holding. That's what it is. I'm afraid to do that. Afraid all my insides will come out. That's why I push hard, then let go. With my knees only a little apart. *Sit like a lady, close your legs,* whenever I wore a dress. All my life I've been taught to keep my knees together, but the real things a woman does, the loving and giving life, these must be done with spread legs. Unladylike. I never was good at being a lady. Not feminine. Female! Being female is spreading my legs, groaning and sweating, making love or giving birth. Sounds the same. Labor the same. Taking Ken in, holding, gripping, squeezing, and now . . . now giving life, bearing down to force everything out, the baby, the water, the blood, and maybe my life. That's what it means to be

Now. A few seconds to get started right. Spread legs. Start a deep, deep breath. Legs fall back together. Grab, push them apart. No good. Get arms outside. Grab under knees, hook arms under the knees, pull back, outward. There, open. Lost my breath, quick, another, pain rising. Now. Bear. Down. Down. Steady. Fire. See flicker! Down—down—FLAME—bear down. Can't hold—can't hold longer—longer—long—pain at the top! Hold! No, out of breath. Another breath? Bear—no, not getting it. Let the pain go down. Let go. Drop legs. Rest. Rest. Close eyes. Let everything go, everything sleep. I think I did better that time. Think so, Friend? I think that was something like what I'm supposed to do. Cold. Wet sheets. Can't move. Have to. Three seconds more rest, then I have to change this sheet. One. Two. Three. Wad it up. Throw it over there. Now reach for the box, raise up a little. Towels on top? They'll do. Get up and—no. Can't. Just raise my bottom a little, slide towels under, all the towels, wad them under me, thick dry pad. Now rest. Rest and sleep. How am I doing, Friend? Not bad that time. Good try for a girl who doesn't know—not a girl. A woman. If I live, I'll be a woman. Good try for a woman who doesn't know what she's doing. Why don't I? I should have listened better when Ken read those books. But I did listen. I should have put them on tape and then—but it still wouldn't matter. Like a man who is taken into the army and is trained to run and jump and fire a gun. But when the real battle comes, what does all his training mean?

When he has to kill or to face death? What was there in his training, in his whole life, to get him ready for that test? To give him courage? Nothing. Some things just come and no preparation can be really like what comes. Like giving birth. Like dying. And sometimes you're not told, you don't know that the test is coming or even that there is such a thing as

Head up. Find a flame—there's one, hold on to it. Legs—wider—hold. Now breathe . . . slow . . . long. More air . . . more . . . deep. Now. Bear down. Bear. Down. Bear. Down. Don't bite lip—keep mouth loose—grunts—groan—am I making all that noise? No one else. Don't waste air on moaning—need more—lost breath—quick breath, now bear—down—open—out—better—pain less? No, but it feels better to—bear—down. Going. . . going . . . keep bearing till—going. Let go. Breathe. Breathe. Breathe. Labor. Now I know why they call it labor. In old stories, in the Bible, they say, she travailled. That's more like it. Harder than labor. Travail. Pain—struggle—labor is travail. Pain and labor tied together, one needing the other. Better when I . . . travail. Pain isn't less, but it's . . . a better pain? Yet. Yet the work, the labor, the bearing down is terrible. Wears me out more than the pain. Harder than the pain. I would rather just have the pain than have to do this labor. Silently endure the pain, rather than labor to push it out. Rather suffer than labor. Oh, Friend, don't frown at me for thinking that. Don't despise me. I despise myself for thinking that, for preferring pain to work. *Passive. Let them walk all over you!* Evelyn. I feel you so close. With my Friend. Our Friend. Right here with me. *Yeah, it's a lot easier to just swallow pain, play dead, be dead, than to do something, be alive!* Evelyn. Something does last after we die. Now I know it. I feel Evelyn. Why not before? Why didn't I ever . . . is it because I'm closer to her? Because I'm going to . . . die? Before I even start to

Head up. Eyes open. A flame —where is a flame! Can't see a streak. Legs up—breathe—where's fire? Breathe. Slow push—hold—hold—hold—fire out? No, warm, still warm—hold —oh, too long to hold—hold—no flame to watch, only smoldering coals. Hold—Hold—oh, help me—no more, please—hold. I can't—yes, hold. Less? No, still coming! Hold—need help—fire—how can it—bear —down—how—last so long—don't want to do this—not alone like this—grunting—whining—animal sounds like—like a woman! This! This . . . less . . . less . . . is woman. This! No. Don't want to . . . fading. Don't want to do this. Want someone else to—who? Let go. Fall. Lean back, fall, fall a mile. Arms loose, legs loose. Panting. Slow. Easy breath. Sweat running, running rivers all over, down my face, neck, legs. Shirt soaked. I held one breath through that whole pain. One breath and one steady bearing down. Pretty good. But I can't do that again. Impossible. No. No, I couldn't do that again. But I'll have to. No, no, no. My heart will stop, my lungs will burst, my body will rip open, my brain will—lips so dry. Where's the cup? Here. Just a sip, just wet lips, smear water, sweat over my lips. More? No, might vomit. Just enough to wet my mouth so that —but it's not fair to expect me to do that again! How many more times? Not fair. No wonder women die. At the hospital they'd help, they'd do something. Forceps. Pain killers. And yet. Yet I would still have to do this alone. With all their help . . . still alone. I never had to do anything myself . . . alone . . . all the way. Never. I didn't really understand that this was all . . . all mine to do. Even in the hospital I would still bear down . . . bear the baby, just as I carried it all these months. Me. I would still have to give my baby life. Never before. No, there was never in my life anything like this, to face alone, to do alone, all

Head up. Eyes open. Arms hook legs, pull wide. Wider. Breathe. Nothing for eyes to see, no flame. Breathe! Push—hold—down—eyes wide open to nothing—darkness—there, a spurt of flame! Gone—hold down—down—no sight—just bearing down in silence with—can't believe this—no, hold it—what's the good? Not enough air—hold the push while I breathe? Impossible! Possible. Hold, breathe, yes—keep pushing the pain—don't let it—fight it, no, don't fight! Just push and hold and steadily shove that pain—going . . . sneaking away . . . shrinking. Can't believe—keep the pushing . . . no, no more. Flop. Dead. Body dead. Fallen. Eyes fallen open. Close. Closed. Dead. Breathe. All of this is impossible. This can't be normal. My body, slick and slippery, dead, quivering like a dying fish, quiver, jerk, dead, dead, quiver. Not dead, mind racing. Shaking. Shocked. My mind spins, spun dizzy with questions. How could all this be? How could all the people in the world be born this way? Nothing in the world as hard as this, not even dying. I don't know about dying, but maybe I'll find out. Maybe I'll do both this and dying, life and death, all at the same time. Like those women in the old cemetery. To do this and then die. Cruel. Unreal. Nothing real but the pain.

It's the world. The pain is the universe. It takes, swallows everything. The pain wants all my strength, my sweat, my grunting and straining. It wants me to help it tear me open, tear out the life that is in me, then tear out my own life. And when I see this, when I know it . . . then it creeps away and hides. Quiet. Nothing. Nowhere. Where is it? How can it—it knows my mind will say, Impossible! Shocked, stunned, my mind, not able to believe it was here. Then it will come back, it will fill the whole universe. Dizzy, my poor mind is spinning off, away, ready to leave me, leave . . . it almost did the last time, at the top of the last pain. And if it spins away, will it come back with the pain? Or will it

No! Coming back, starting again. Oh, Friend, help me. Help me get away. I can't do it. Grab legs. Slippery. I can't! Breathe. Can't! Help me! I'm a coward, can't do this. Push! No, I've got to get away. Escape! Someone. Friend, help me get away! Push! No, not me, not my mind. I'm running away, I'm escaping. Leave this body—pushing—pushing—no, I won't come back! Let me go. Going! Help! Coward. Giving up. A coward. Go where? I can't go. It's going. Pain going for now. But not me. I can't go anywhere. I can admit I'm a coward but I can't go. Not like the soldier. He can desert when the test comes. Turn and run. Disgrace, guilt, shame, but safety. Not me. I have no choice. Coward or not, I have to do it. No medals. No one caring about whether or not I was brave. Don't tell about it, not like the man in battle. No one wants to hear. Old wives' tales. Disgusting. Women talking about childbirth, disgusting. Men talking about killing, exciting. Giving life is messy.

No glory, no dignity, no heroism. Just bare-assed grunting and pushing. No one wants to hear about it. That's why Mom never . . . three times. And no one cared. No medals. No wonder she didn't really want us. Sorry, Mom. No right to judge you. Not until I see how I do, if I live. I don't think I will, Mom. But if I do, I start out different, knowing. I start out knowing you better. Three times. And you weren't any older than I am and knew less, maybe. So you did your best with what you had, a kid yourself, doing your best, trying to grow up with three of us ripping out of you and hanging off you, weighing you down. You tried to love us. As much as you could, the way you could. Dad too? Even Dad? Next to this travail tearing me, forgiving Dad doesn't seem hard. Like nothing. Easy to forgive him. Stuck with babies to support, wife, family, house. Stuck. Maybe he should have been an explorer, climbed mountains, wandered through deserts, sailed oceans. That's why he was so restless. Chained, stuck to a life he couldn't leave, stuck to us. Poor Dad. Poor Mom. Poor

Will it kill me this time? Yes. Try anyway. Die trying. Head up. Eyes open. Nothing to see. Log only smoldering. Eyes open anyway as if I could see. Alert. Arms hook legs—breathe—breathe—bear—down—bear—down—down—match you, pain—match pain with push—who is the stronger? No, concentrate—hold—hold—no thoughts—push—out of body—out of mind—hold—hold. So afraid! Here comes—the worst—hold—breathe, but keep bearing down, open, pushing—hold—pain going! Still hold—chase after it—follow pain—with—pushing—hold—no more. Can't. Loose, let go, fall. Breathe. Breathe. Breathe. Still alive! A miracle. I'm stronger than I thought I was. Much stronger. It'll take a few more like that before I—Evelyn? How was that? Better? Not brave like you, but there just doesn't seem to be much point in being afraid. Can't run away, can't stop it from coming back. Not dying bravely like you, knowing it all the time and living so well. I'm just . . . maybe-dying. Maybe. Can't think. Mind muddle. Bits of my mind fly off with each pain and don't come back. Mind in shreds. Soft, sagging, soggy, limp shreds left. Maybe the brain dies first and then the body. But what stays alive? Evelyn? What is left of you that's here with me? Are you just in my imagination? Shreds of a mind that—all right, if so, all right, then that's where you live. You live. And Ken? Where is

Beginning. Don't think of Ken. Get ready. Breathe deep. All automatic now. Breath. Head. Eyes. Arms. Legs. No thoughts. No brain. Breathe—bear—down—hold, head up—hold, eyes open—hold seeing nothing—hold legs, hold while I breathe again. Hold to the pain—with the pain—against the pain—hold away fear—hold—hold—hold—HOLD! Quick breath while it sinks—hold a little longer. Let go. Drop. Breathe and die. No thoughts. Mind gone. Nothing. Empty. Ken? So my mind isn't all gone. I remember Ken. No more anger at Ken. So angry I forgot all the good, the good now all coming back. Are you here, Ken? With Evelyn? Is Ken dying too, dead, at the bottom of the canyon under the jeep? No, no, not both of us. The baby will need someone. This baby, I'm going to get it born, no matter what happens to me, so Ken, please don't be dead. For the sake of baby, for your own sake, for my sake, be drunk, passed out, safe with Marge and Burt, safe and quiet and sleeping. Be alive. In case I die. And . . . if I don't die . . . be safe. For all of us. Because nothing has changed. If I don't die, I'll forgive, I've already forgiven, forgotten it all, thrown away with shreds of mind I won't need anymore. It doesn't matter, it's all an accident, something you couldn't help. Like Mom and Dad. Like everyone we know. Like me. I'm a coward and I can't help it. I'm just doing the best I can. Just the way everyone does. Everyone does! Imagine! Everyone does . . . the best they can do. Isn't that beautiful? Did you know that, Friend? Sure you did, you're telling me . . . telling me such a beautiful truth because the truth is so restful, so soothing, and gives me such peaceful, restful

One more time. Try—try—one more good push—for the baby—before—one more—how? Quick, pain rising fast. Head—grab legs—breathe—bear down—hold—try—trying! So tired. Don't let go, hold on—Friend? Help me. Please help. No—not to escape—not to take the pain away—no—just help me—hold—help me hold with the pain, help—me—get—this—baby—out—before—I die—hold! Can't. Falling. Falling . . . fallen. Pain still going down. Down. Pain won that time. Outlasted me. I couldn't hold anymore. I tried. I held and held in my mind but my body couldn't. It just gave out. I smell blood. How much? Can't tell. How long does it take to bleed to death? How much time to get the baby out? How much strength? Rest. Rest for the next one. Do my best. That's all, Friend. Like everyone else, I can only do . . . my best. Still here? Don't leave me alone now. Stay, Friend. That's all, just stay. Not asking you to save my life, save the baby, save—no, not asking for anything anymore. Just asking—whatever is, whatever happens, if you'll stay with me I'll keep trying, push with the pain, join the pain. Nothing left, no strength left to push, but I'll try anyway. I promise. Until the end. No saying no. Yes. Saying yes. If that's what you want, I'll try. Just stay with

Yes, here it comes. Yes, I'll try—try—breathe—arms loop legs—can't. Try. I promise—arms too tired to—got them, hold. Lost breath. Friend, hold me. Good. Yes, yes, another breath. Start to push. No strength left? Yes—yes—there is more—push—where does the strength come from? From you, Friend? Never thought—don't think—push—hold—bear down—more—more strength—there is always more—the last—all—all gone? More than I—pain still rising? Hold—rising—another breath while I hold—am I holding? Bearing down? Feel nothing. Know nothing. Pain and no pain. Feel no difference between pain and no pain. And holding. Holding? I'm still trying, Friend, but I don't know what I'm doing. Pain gone? Fallen. Fallen. All in shreds. Mind. Body. Can't feel my body anymore. Can't do anymore. Something in me will keep trying, but not my body, not my mind, all collapsed, all in shreds, all. I told Ken he was wrong, I was only big, not strong like he said. I hope he'll forgive me. You'll forgive me? Friend? Already forgiven? I failed. No? Didn't I fail to

Already? Breathe—breathe—head up—legs, no, arms—arms hook legs—breathe—fold into push against pain—grows too fast—don't think, just—

press—bear—down—coming to the top—already—no, oh, no. Legs falling . . . falling . . . breath gone, gone. Can't. Limp. Can't make my body . . . all, Friend. I've done all I can. Nothing will move, nothing will—burning. Burning? Pain burns me. Pain on fire. I'm on fire? Giving birth to fire. Bursting open, burning sharp. And fallen. My body is dead, fallen. So it's the body that dies first, not the mind. I couldn't move again. Arms. Legs. Head. Eyes. No strength left to lift eyelids when the next pain comes. Nothing left. Body squeezed dry of everything, feeling nothing except that burning sensation, as if another fire will take me, like a log, a fallen, dead log. Smoldering. Burning. Flames make light. Light? Growing. I see light. Not seeing, not with my eyes, but the light grows, all around, glowing like the flame, around me, in me. The light and I burning—no pain—burning brightness—not burning—warming, loving. Light loving me, warm. Friend! You're beautiful. Beautiful. Fading. I fall and fade away from the light. Thank you, Friend, for showing me your light before . . . I fade . . . fade . . . fall and fade. I'm dying. That's what the light means. Fading light. Fading. Can't have the light without dying. Dying. All right. I'm happy. My body is dead. My mind lives for a little while longer. My mind filled with light. White, bright. Now it's fading too. Fading to gold. Gold going dark, fading with me. How lovely, Friend, to fade with the light . . . into your light . . . all fading together, all sinking. Dying. All pain gone now. Only the warm glow from the light my eyes could never see, even when they could see, lighting up every cell, every atom of me. Inside and outside, loving me and folding me up inside itself. So that I am all light. Fading as my mind is fading. All flickering out like a fire dying, glowing out like a sun sinking. That's all it is, just sinking into the light and fading with it. All fading, going, fading down to darkness. Darker. Deepest, blackest dark. Dark.

Crying.

Crying? Who's crying? Somewhere a baby is—what? Muffled crying. A baby. What is touching my thigh? Baby! The baby's head. Oh, don't cry, don't cry. Here, let me—poor little face, face down on the wet sheets. Here, I'll hold your little face up. I'll hold you. There. There, I'm holding your head, won't let it drop, my hand between your face and the sheets. Little, slippery, soft head. Crying, crying. Are you afraid? Out in a strange place and can't see where you are? Oh, I can't see either and it's not so bad. Nothing to be afraid of. I'm here with you. Always. Still holding you, not inside anymore, but I'll hold you outside, keep you safe. I promise. That's it. Easy.

Oh, you can hear me, can't you? Quiet, listening to me. You know it's . . . your mother. Now, just wait, be patient and pretty soon there'll be another squeeze and you'll be all the way out. Don't worry, you won't fall. I'll hold you, I promise, never let you fall. Yes, all right, cry again a little if you want to, so I hear how strong you are.

Now. Listen, dear. It's starting now. Another squeeze is coming and I have to stop talking. Don't be afraid. I'm going to push you out. I won't let go. This hand holding your head, the other ready to hold the rest of you, just let you ease out into my hands. It'll hurt us a little but only for a minute. I'll cry a little too. Don't worry. Don't be afraid. Now. Breathe. One—more — steady — even — bearing — down — coming — easy — slipping—sliding—out!

Here. Here's a dry towel under you. There. Turn you over. There. Resting, rest there between Mother's legs. Safe. Rest while I rest for just a minute. Okay, cry if you want, but just don't be afraid. I'm here. I'm just resting here for a little while. You're not lost. We're still together, still tied together. Can't pick you up yet. Cord too short. Let me catch my breath. Rest. There. There.

Now. Let Mother see you. Touch you. Little head. Felt like a mountain coming out! But so little, soft on top and . . . with hair! Soft, wet, slippery hair, long . . . coming down over your ears. Tiny, perfect little curls of ears. Eyelids, open eyes, blink. Want to see? Want to see right away. Can you see Mother? No, not yet. Only some light and shadow. Like me. For a little while, we're the same, not seeing each other, meeting in the dark, how do you do? Later you'll see everything and tell Mother what you see. Nose. Oh, so soft and little. But a great, wide mouth, crying again. Stopping as I touch your mouth, funny, quick little mouth, feeling, tasting, sucking at my fingers.

Neck? No neck at all. Little head set on little body with nothing in between, like a little old—let me feel your little chest, back, all around. Oh, you like that, you're so quiet, feeling Mother feeling you, down your stomach to sex.

Girl! Margaret. Maggie. Little Maggie, we named you after a great, fine little lady.

Legs. Curled up little legs. Tiny feet. Tiny toes. Oh, such tiny toes, tiny toenails, how can anyone feel such tiny toes and not cry? Arms. Waving strong arms. Long fingers, strong, thin, long fingers, grabbing, holding my finger while I rub your funny big round little belly. The place where we are still connected, you and I, still beating heartbeats together, the cord beating and beating. No, it's stopping now, getting longer and limp and stopping. Our rhythm won't be the same anymore. We'll be two separate people. Should I cut us apart now? No, the fire's only coals now, can't clean the knife in the fire. No, we'll stay together, tied together a while longer. Cord getting longer, longer. Soon the place where it connects you to me will let go, let go of me.

I feel it, feel pain starting, the last squeezing out, pushing out the connection between us, what has held you inside me and fed you and brought everything from me into you, my blood to yours, our blood. Oh, that hurts more, more, the pain of letting go, separating us.

Oh, no, I couldn't let go of you. Not ever. Part of me. Part of my body, beat of my heartbeat. Even though this cord is letting go of me . . . always, where-ever you are, always an invisible cord between us. Oh, poor little Maggie, I'm sorry, forgive your mother for all the dumb, stupid worrying I'll do, for the fear I'll try to hide, fear of letting you go where I can't touch you, can't stroke and rub you like this, can't protect your precious tiny toes.

There. It's out. You're not part of me anymore. But you're not leaving me yet. You still need me for a long time yet.

And now I can hold you. Up. Yes, I'll hold your wobbly little head, bring you up to me, up to Mother, close to me, skin to skin. Yes, come up to Mother's breast, shirt open, under Mother's shirt. What . . . well, I don't know just how to do this either. Both of us trying but. . .let me touch your little mouth. Yes. there it is. But don't suck my fingers. Mother has something better. Here. Taste . . . is that right? Are we . . . try to . . .

I did it! We did it! There you are sucking away as if we've been doing this forever. Oh, isn't that fine, doesn't that feel good. My baby, my Margaret. Let's just lean back now. Here's a blanket for us, a big, soft shawl from Spain, a shawl with a history. I'll tell you the whole story of it. Later. For now we'll just rest, rest while you take Mother's breast. We'll just pull this shawl over us both while I close my eyes and rest, rest the most delicious rest ever. Most beautiful . . . peaceful . . . rest.

Someone calling me? Another dream?

Someone coming? A car. Not the jeep. Ken's voice? No jeep, can't be Ken. Baby? Did I dream? No. Baby! Margaret. Here. Daylight, no more dark. Sun streaming through the window, all over us. Warm. Margaret, your first day. Not sucking. Asleep. Asleep in my arms. We slept.

'Lon!'

Yes, it is Ken! Running up the path. Your father. Sleep. Later you'll see . . .

'Lon? You must have been frantic. I had—I thought I'd never get—oh, Jesus! Oh, my God! Lon!'

'I'm all right, Ken. It's all right. I'm perfectly fine. And the baby too. See? A little girl. Tell me how she looks. Is she beautiful? What color hair? She's all sticky, but—isn't she beautiful!'

'Oh, Lon. Yes. Yes. Beautiful. You—my God—alone. You're all right? Oh, my God. Lon . . . '

'All right. Yes, all right. Don't cry, Ken.'

'The rain . . . when it started, I tried to hurry back . . . jeep went off the road . . . knocked out . . . '

'What's this? A cast. Your arm? Broken?'

'Just my wrist . . . came to . . . had to walk . . . picked me up . . . hospital . . . are you sure you're all right? I made them lend me a car as soon as . . . road washed out . . . had to come clear around the ridge road. Oh, Lon, you must have . . . '

'Your wrist? What else?'

'Nothing . . . doesn't matter. Just . . . if you're all right.'

'I'm fine. Oh, there she goes. Hasn't she got a strong, good cry. And me too. Oh, how silly, now we're all crying, all three of us. How funny. Crying and laughing. That's it, Ken. Laugh. I'm all right. In a minute you can help me get up. We'll go to the hospital. Sure, I can ride. I feel fine. I just had a wonderful nap. Where are you going? Don't . . . '

'Just checking. Not much blood. I'll have to cut the cord. No, I'll wrap everything up with the baby. The doctor will want to see the placenta. Water. Here, drink some water.'

'Yes.' Yes, take over, Ken. Capable, dependable Ken. Take care of us. I did it all alone, enough alone, now let you take care of us.

'Give me the baby, Lon. Then I'll get you fixed up. I'll wet some towels and wash you up, then . . . '

'No, wait. In a minute. Come close again, Ken. Sit down here with us. Touching me. Close. Things I want to tell you. Hold me. Hold us. Arms around us both. That's right, that's just right. Let's just stay here together, all three of us, touching, for a little while. I want to tell you what happened. Everything. Not just the pain and the labor. Not just the fear. I was afraid, but I was brave too. Not just that. All the rest too. All the thoughts that came to me, the waves of thoughts, new waves rolling over old waves, blending and changing. Let's just sit here nice and warm in the sunlight and I'll tell you. So many things. I knew. I knew so many things. I understood everything—everything, so clearly. But now it's all beginning to fade. I'm starting to forget all the things I learned. So let me tell you before I lose it all.

'First of all, you were right about me, Ken. I won't forget that. You were right. I *am* strong. I can do . . . anything!'